About the author

Guy Philip Evans grew up on the edge of East London in Barking where he spent most of his childhood immersed in books, cartoons of the 1980s and imaginary battles with his friends, not realising the huge wodge of history just sitting on his doorstep. He does now! Guy studied English and Drama at St Mary's University, Strawberry Hill and is a qualified teacher. He is a massive fantasy and sci-fi geek, which he hopes comes out in his first book.

THE LOST CHRONICLES OF EAST LONDON: THE STREETS OF DARKNESS

Happy Reading! :)

Guy Evans

THE LOST CHRONICLES OF EAST LONDON: THE STREETS OF DARKNESS

Vanguard Press

A CIP catalogue record for this title is
available from the British Library.

ISBN 978 1 784658 71 7

*Vanguard Press is an imprint of
Pegasus Elliot MacKenzie Publishers Ltd.*
www.pegasuspublishers.com

First Published in 2020

**Vanguard Press
Sheraton House Castle Park
Cambridge England**

Printed & Bound in Great Britain

THE STREETS OF DARKNESS

The entity had existed for millennia in one form or another. Once it had been free to walk the universe consuming all in its path for its own amusement, feeding on the fear and hatred that it caused. Until it had been bound, seemingly for all eternity, on a world that was still young. A world that was full of promise. It had been drawn to it irresistibly, like a moth to a flame. And there it had resided until it had attempted to destroy this world completely. But it hadn't counted on the people of the world it had entered. They wanted life, not death, and bound it with deep magic and powerful incantations within the stones of an ancient city where it could not escape. There it could only watch and fester as the city grew up around it, becoming larger and more important as it did so, eventually becoming the most powerful city of them all, at the heart of the most influential empire the world had ever seen.

The thing watched as, even without its influence, the people of the city were divided by circumstance. Rich and poor, strong and weak, mingling together in a melting pot that was both prosperous and the very image of poverty. It was within these streets, in the eastern quarter of the city, that the thing was bound. But the feelings and emotions of those that dwelled in those cramped and dirty alleys and courtyards gave it purpose and renewed strength and it struck out as best it could many times, causing misery and fear, but never able to show its full power.

And it was so, in the East End of London, towards the end of the 19th century, when things that were at their very worst for those that lived there despite the wealth and power that surrounded them, that the entity saw a chance: a chance for renewed freedom and to begin again its reign of eternal darkness.

CHAPTER ONE
THE SIGN OF THE BELL

Joe stared out of the window, watching the rain hammering down onto the dirty pane, collecting in grubby puddles at the bottom, and wondered how long until the bell would ring for the end of the lesson. How could time go so slowly when he was at school and so fast when he was laying on the sofa watching rubbish on TV? He was bored, so very, very bored. He hated history. He hated school. He hated this school. He wanted to go home.

He picked at the corner of his exercise book, flaking the paper into small flecks and rolling them up into tiny balls which he dropped on the floor underneath the desk.

"Joe Druitt!"

The loud, harsh voice that rang in his ears dragged him out of his misery. Joe turned his head to see the towering form of Mr Lusk, his loathed history teacher, resplendent in a hideous brown-and-orange-check suit resembling the seat of a London bus, bearing down on him.

"You haven't listened to a single word I've been saying all lesson, have you?" The massive bearded face thrust itself close to his and Joe could smell the aroma of stale staffroom coffee and what had obviously been last night's curry. He wrinkled his nose.

The man could at least have brushed his teeth if he wants to get that close, the boy thought to himself, *and no wonder he's not married.*

"No." The word was out of his mouth before he could stop himself. Joe felt himself go red and wished he'd allowed his dark hair to grow so that it would cover his face. He heard the giggles and snorts that came from the rest of the class but didn't react. Joe was used to them laughing at him. Everyone laughed at him. Out of the corner of his eye he could see Lusk's face turning a mottled purple colour, like an overripe grape floating in a sea of matted hair.

"I see…if the history of your own country holds no interest for you, then you can go."

Mr Lusk's voice had taken on a dangerous edge and the corners of his mouth had turned upwards which always signified trouble to the pupils.

"What?" Joe couldn't believe what he was hearing. There had to be some catch. Lusk was not known for his kindness. He had been known to make younger pupils wet themselves out of spite.

"You may go," repeated the history teacher, "although I would like an essay on the state of London's East End at the end of the 19th century by next Monday, if you please. Shall we say 2000 words so you can really show what you can do? Class dismissed."

Joe felt his jaw drop to the ground and stared in dismay at Mr Lusk's smug, retreating form and the laughing, open mouths of his classmates and then slumped his head forward with a dismal crash onto the desk.

"Nice one, meat head!"

***

12

Joe tried to ignore the bright and cheerful voice that greeted him as he mooched moodily down the school steps on his way home.

"Oi! Meat head! How are ya gonna get it done? You can't even string two words together, let alone a sentence. You. Are. Screwed!"

Joe turned angrily to see Florence Kelly leaning nonchalantly against a pillar, smiling at him with round dark eyes. The eyes seemed to be laughing at him. Joe had often thought she would be pretty if her mouth wasn't so hard.

She had a pale complexion with strawberry blonde hair; every schoolboy's dream…if she wasn't such a cow and her face wasn't smothered in goth makeup and her skirt wasn't masquerading as a belt.

"Shut it, Kelly. At least I'm not a flamin' moron like you."

"What? Cos I actually care about leaving school with something other than my dole book? Oh, I forgot—you can't actually read!" Her voice was mocking, which to the enraged boy was like a red rag to a bull.

Joe felt his face go even redder and saw from the look on Flo's face that she knew she had gone too far. She began to backtrack, stammering hopelessly, but it was too late for Flo now. Joe had had enough of taunts and jibes for one day and now he had been tipped over the edge.

She could see his hands ball into fists and she started edging away nervously whilst trying to apologise, but the boy wasn't having any of it. "Look, that was mean. I'm sorry. I know that you—"

"You know nothing!" Joe was marching angrily towards her, arms swinging dangerously. He was a tall boy for his age and she, being rather short, backed away. "You know nothing about me or my life. But what do you care? You seem to exist only to make everyone feel like rubbish! But, hey, I suppose that since no one here actually likes you, weirdo goth-girl, it's the only thing you can do. Now get out of my way."

Pushing the startled girl against the wall, Joe stormed angrily back in the opposite direction. He realised he'd gone the wrong way, kicked open the side fire door, and marched out across the wet playground. Flo stared after the back of the retreating boy until the fire door snapped shut.

"What did you have to do that for?" sighed an exasperated voice that made Flo jump. "Don't you know how he feels about his family? And that he can't read?"

Edward Eddows, who had been watching the argument from the shadows, laid a calming hand on Flo's trembling shoulder. "You can't do that with him, you know that. He has…issues."

"Like what?"

***

Joe stopped walking when he felt he was far enough away from school not to be seen. He sat down hard on a seat at the nearest bus stop, breathed heavily a few times and then wiped the hot, bitter and angry tears from his eyes. He really felt like he could strangle Flo! Stupid goth girl. She knew nothing about him or what life had been like for him. Nobody did. Nobody had any idea what life was like for him. Nobody. All right, so he couldn't read very well but he wasn't thick. He'd show her. He'd show them all. It couldn't be that hard to write about the East End, could it? After all, that was where he had lived all his life.

He stood up and looked around. He realised that he'd been so angry he hadn't bothered to look where he had been going or just how heavy the rain was. He was soaked and now he was lost. Humiliated, soaked and lost. Joe looked around and could just about make out the Canary Wharf tower through the mist and rain and some other buildings on the horizon beyond.

Joe sighed and breathed hard, trying to calm himself down. He noticed that the bus shelter had a map on the glass wall and he stared at it, trying to make some sense of it. The numbers and letters seemed to swirl and slide around over the map, change shape even, becoming something else altogether. He might as well have been reading Arabic. For all he knew, he was.

The rain, which was hammering hard as bullets on the shelter roof, made his efforts at trying to read the name of the street on the bus map even more difficult.

Focussing hard, Joe tried putting all the sounds together. Co-mm-er-cial Ro-ad, Commercial Road, that was it. The main road to the centre of London. He watched the traffic go past, cars and lorries, headlights reflecting the rain bouncing on the ground, throwing up the mud and rubbish that was London in the middle of the wettest winter the boy could remember. At least he had some idea of where he was now. But what would be the quickest, and more importantly, driest way home? Joe looked at the map and the words that jumped and danced before his eyes, blinked heavily and then gave up.

Shrugging his shoulders with resignation, Joe set off once again into the deluge and taking an executive decision, turned right down a side street, where shop awnings would give at least some shelter from the rain.

A pub stood on the corner of one of the side streets. A very old and very unremarkable East End of London pub. He could, with an effort, read the name: The Ten Bells. This made sense judging from the sign showing ten bells outside. Brown peeling paint and dirty windows were thrown more sharply into focus with the driving rain. Joe caught a faint glimpse of a warm, orange light glowing through the steamy window. The wind picked up and rain was thrown, as if by invisible hands, into his face. The pub seemed to shimmer, like a mirage, as he wiped the wet droplets from his cold face.

Joe made a decision. He would ask the landlord where he was and how he might get back home. If he played it right, he might even be given something warm, too. What would be the harm in playing the lost little boy card?

Joe started to cross the road towards the pub when a car made him swerve to one side and he found himself stood at the corner of a disused service road, with a view of a small car park to one side.

Within its prison of stone, the entity stirred, stretching out shadows that billowed like black ribbons. If it had had hands it would have rubbed them together. The first of his Contracts had fallen, satisfying but little challenge. It could feel already the rising panic and fear among those it was surrounded by and it was glad. The Game had now begun. *Let them think they stand a chance*, the entity thought. *Let them think they have a hope, a future. Let the mouse see the cat and let the next fall...*

It was at that moment that Joe felt sick. The ground beneath his feet seemed to lurch up and he felt himself fall forward as if into nothingness. Darkness welled up in front of him, a thick, smothering darkness that seemed to be all encompassing. And then he felt the wind and rain again, only this time it felt colder and seemed to pluck at his face and clothes with a vengeance. Joe held his hands up to try and feel ahead of him. The car park swam into view.

His vision seemed to narrow until all that he could see was that desolate car park which seemed more menacing and darker than before. It appeared to grow before his aching eyes until it consumed his whole view.

And yet it seemed to be changing form…it seemed to be shaping itself into a long-forgotten picture of what once had been but was no longer. It pushed out arms that spread over the road into dark narrow passages that had never seen sunlight, into decaying courtyards that seemed to shun the day and into old, rancid-looking, grubby houses that seemed to crowd into each other as if for support. The shapes appeared to crawl grotesquely before Joe's eyes as if the very houses were cruelly alive. Like rats crawling over a corpse.

Joe reached out with grasping hands to steady himself. As his feeling of nausea grew, he felt himself retch and choke. Noise and sound pounded in his ears, indistinguishable at first, just a multitude of noise. It became louder and the boy clamped his hands hard over his ears as the sound of bells pealed forth and the cries of "Murder! Ripper!" rent the air. Joe felt as if his head would burst before he slipped into merciful oblivion.

***

"Wake up, lad! Come on now. That's it." The voice in his ears seemed to come from far away, as if down a long tunnel.

17

Joe found himself laid on the floor in the pub he had been standing outside, with concerned faces looking up at him. Helped by kind hands, he slowly sat up. Joe felt as if his body had been worked over with sticks; every small movement was agony.

"Where am I?" he managed to croak. His mouth felt hot, dry, and unpleasant and his eyes were having trouble focussing on the sea of concerned faces around him. The faces seemed to swim before him. *I wonder if this is what it's like to be drunk*, he thought to himself.

"The Ten Bells Public House. We found you on the street outside. Sopping wet you were. Completely out of it." A fat, rough-looking man helped him to sit up. A woman in a pink top and too-tight jeans wrapped a warm, dry blanket around his shoulders and Joe managed to give her a grateful smile.

"I must have fainted. I felt so sick, must have passed out." Joe knew he hadn't but didn't want to appear nuts in front of people he didn't know. "Thanks for looking after me. I feel better now."

He tried to stand but his legs felt as if they had been turned to jelly and he sat back down heavily.

"Whoa! Slow down, boy. You've been out for a while now. Here, let me phone your parents. They'll be worried about you." The man tried to lay Joe down again.

"No!" shouted Joe and he struggled to his feet despite the man's pleas for him to lay back down. Startled, the man turned to the woman for support.

"My parents… They work nights. They won't be home," Joe managed to blurt out. "Just call me a cab and I'll get home. My nan's in, but deaf as a post and she won't hear the phone. Please."

The man, looking a little less concerned now from Joe's explanation, gave a bemused glance at his lady friend, who shrugged her shoulders in resignation, went out the back of the pub to call the taxi.

An awkward silence followed. Joe looked about him. The pub was as dingy inside as it had been outside. Nicotine-stained walls and ceilings, coloured brown from years of cigarette smoke. These were complemented by some ornate lead-lined glass windows and ten small brass bells above the bar, some worn sofas, grudgingly stuffed, and some very old and notched bar stools on which sat the equally battered patrons of the pub. There was the quiet chinking of glasses.

One item stood out as if it shouldn't be there. It looked to Joe as if it was some kind of a roll of honour with very few names on it—although this being the rough end of the East End of London—that didn't surprise him.

"What's that?" he asked, pointing to the names on the wall and winced as his arm responded stiffly to the unwelcome movement. He felt a little surprised and foolish when the man started to laugh. Joe felt his face begin to redden again. Laughed at again. *It had been a crap day all round*, he thought.

"You mean you don't know?" The man sounded surprised. "You live 'ere and you don't know?"

"I can't read," Joe snapped back and felt vaguely pleased to see the man stop laughing. "Just tell me what it is. No, don't. Just read the names to me."

"All right, boy. I didn't mean to upset you," said the man gently, making Joe feel a little guilty for his outburst. He was about to reply when another voice cut in, rich and deep. It sounded strange among the Cockney voices he had heard so far.

"I suppose the one name you might have heard of is Mary Kelly."

Joe turned and saw in the shadows the shape of a man sat at one of the tables. The form seemed hazy in the dingy light of the pub, although the man's eyes seemed to stand out, green, against the gloom. They reminded Joe of a cat. A gust of wind blew through the pub door and one of the bells on the wall rang gently as if pushed by some invisible force.

CHAPTER TWO
THE STREET

Joe suddenly felt sick again and his head was swimming. The name seemed to reverberate through his head over and over again, but he didn't know why. He had heard of the name before but after admitting that he couldn't read he wasn't going to let on that he didn't know who this 'Mary Kelly' person was.

"Course I've heard of her. She's famous, isn't she?" He hoped that the vagueness of his answer would make the man talk some more. Instead the man just nodded his head and muttered under his breath, "Yes. Yes, she is—was, considering what she was and where she was living."

"What she was?" queried Joe.

"Let's just say, like most of us, she did things she shouldn't have."

The man at the table turned away and looked out of the grubby window at the jumble of the crowded city beyond. "I know it seems difficult to believe, but some of London was even worse than it is now. A hundred years or so ago this city was a very different place." The voice sounded as if it had lived it.

The woman returned. "Cab's on its way. Will be here shortly. You feeling better?" She seemed to not be aware of the other man at the table.

"Yes. Thanks. That road you found me on?"

21

Joe felt that he should ask. He didn't know why but felt that it was important he should know.

"Oh, that. It don't really have a name." The woman shifted uneasily on the balls of her feet, as if not wanting to be there.

"It used to be called Dorset Street before it was knocked down about 40 years ago to make that car park thing. Not that there was much to knock down. You could have blown it over, the state it was in. The council said it might knock some of the crime down too. If anything, it's the worst car park in London. Ironic really."

"Ironic?" Joe was intrigued now. He felt as if something was calling to him, close but far away, tinkling in the back of his mind like the bells that had rung on the pub wall.

"Yeah. Dorset Street," the fat man answered. "Was said by the police to be the worst street in London. Crime, poverty, filth, ladies of the night…"

"Fred! Stop it!" The lady interrupted the man sharply. "The boy don't need to know all this. He's only…how old are you anyway?" Her voice softened slightly as she looked down at the bedraggled schoolboy.

"Fourteen," answered Joe.

He was annoyed. He wanted to know more. Joe felt he had to know more. He wanted to know everything that there was to know about this "Dorset Street."

They heard a car drawing up outside the pub, followed by the loud hooting of a horn. The lady snapped into action and helped Joe to the door, giving the fat man a filthy look as she did. She had half opened the door when the man at the table stood up and grabbed hold of Joe's shoulder and looked him full in the

22

face. The man's expression was serious and, Joe thought, almost frightening. The other man and woman seemed frozen, like dolls.

"Dorset Street, boy. You may think it's gone but it's still there, somewhere out there in the shadows, in the darkness. Like a stain that can never be wiped out. It exists in the mind and spirit of those that lived there. Dorset Street. Remember that name. Mary Kelly did. It drew her in. Like it drew many poor, lost souls who thought their hopes and dreams would come true in this city. It was more of a 'thing' than an 'it' by the end. Maybe now it's drawn you to it."

"What…what do you mean?" Joe whispered.

"There are things about this city, this world, boy, that you can never imagine. You may see more than you should before this night is through."

"I don't understand," Joe stammered. Things were just getting weirder and weirder.

"There is more to you too than you can possibly understand. But the time is not yet right. You are…important."

The green eyes flashed again and Joe saw, for a fleeting second, the universe reflected in their depths and he felt himself falling and his world slip away. Images flashed through his mind. Galaxies, planets and stars whirled through his brain, filling his mind with strange whispers of dark things that shone brighter than the sun. Formless, they reached out to him…

Then Joe was back in the room and time seemed to move again. The lady sprang back to life and moved Joe through the door and into the waiting taxi car. Swinging round, the boy saw that the man at the table had vanished.

***

Joe slammed the front door of the flat behind him and let out a huge sigh. He threw his sodden school bag onto the floor and waded through the obstacle course of rubbish that littered the narrow hallway into the sitting room. Joe hated living like this.

He hated living in this tiny, cramped flat, hated living on the sink estate that lay just outside the door. Hated the fact there seemed to be no way out. Joe cast his eyes around the sitting room. The room looked tired and worn out. Much like he felt.

A cheap leather sofa, a battered TV and DVD player from Spitalfields Market, a dead pot plant fossilising nicely, the old ticking clock on the wall. And Nan.

There was Nan sat in her chair like an old doll. Still. Not moving or talking, staring into space. She'd been like that for as long as Joe had known her. She must have been about 90 but her skin was smooth. White like paper or snow. Her hair was white. Her hands and skin were white apart from the blue veins that threaded over her hands like streams coursing through her body. "Snow White," the man who he had called dad had said before he had left. It was only her eyes, huge and dark like pools, that gave her face any colour at all.

Sometimes, Joe wondered exactly just how old his nan was. There was talk from some of the neighbours that she had lived through both world wars. If that was so, that would make her well over a hundred. But that would be ridiculous. And anyway, Joe reasoned, that would make his mum how old?

"Hello, Nan. Good day? Mum not back yet?" Joe had to talk to her, or he felt he'd go mad. It was strange, but he was sure that she could hear him. He looked at her. Nothing. Nan just staring ahead into the distance. Joe wondered what she was thinking. If she even was thinking and if she was even aware of him? He pressed on regardless.

"I've had a rubbish day at school, Nan. I was caught daydreaming in history by old Lusk. Remember, I told you about him? Nasty suit, big beard like a cut-price Santa? Breath like Satan's armpits? He's making me write an essay on the East End in the 19th century. If you could talk, I'd ask you, Nan. You've lived in the area all your life. I bet you know everything there is to know. Let's face it, you're so old you probably remember it."

Joe took a sideways look at Nan. Nothing. Just the same still form and deep staring eyes. He began to wonder why he even bothered. He tried again.

"Ever heard of Dorset Street?"

Silence. It was oppressive. Joe sighed, shrugged his shoulders and turned to go to into the kitchen for something to eat. He felt hungry after his interesting evening.

"Worst street in London."

Joe spun round. He looked at the old woman in the chair. She had spoken! After all this time! The first words out of her mouth he'd ever heard. Ever! Well, as far back as he could remember. Joe didn't know why but he felt slightly frightened. As if Nan was an ancient treasure that shouldn't be disturbed. Like there might be a curse attached to her. Bit like that boy-mummy he had learned about in junior school.

He'd made a plaster mummy out of wet bandages. He'd even managed to muck that up as he couldn't read the instructions on the board. The only mummy in the class with a hump and no head. Joe narrowed his eyes. He looked closely at Nan. She was as silent as before, staring into space. The sound of the cheap

1970s clock that hung at its odd angle on the wall seemed loud in the silence.

"Say again?" Joe broke the silence.

"Worst street in London."

The voice came again, high and light and almost singing, almost childlike. The sound was cracked and broken through lack of use, reminding Joe of dried leaves.

"Nan? You can talk?"

Nothing. Not a sausage. He looked at her again and felt as if the effort had exhausted her. He watched her eyes close and her head fall gently onto her chest. Joe went over to the tiny figure slumped in the battered armchair. He reached out a hand and gently shook her shoulder. It felt cold, like ice. For a moment, Joe felt his stomach lurch with the thought that maybe the effort to speak had killed her. Then he relaxed as he heard Nan snore. Relieved, but annoyed that twice information about Dorset Street had been denied him, Joe went out to the kitchen to find himself some food.

***

The kitchen was the same state as the hall. Plates, cups and cutlery were piled high in the sink, bringing to mind the Leaning Tower of Pisa. Washing lay in dirty piles on the floor and a stale smell of grease and old fat came wafting from the oven when he opened it. Joe wrinkled his nose and slammed the oven door shut.

"Urgh! It's like a science experiment gone wrong," he muttered to himself. "It's disgusting in here. I could create life…" He picked his way through the mountain of grubby crockery and, performing a delicate balancing act, pulled out a cup. Joe looked with interest at the green and brown mould that had gathered around the base, knew it would take the strength of a pneumatic drill to remove it and dropped it into the bin. He was hungry and thirsty, but his head was whirring. He wanted to know what had happened to him on his way home from school, why the pub had been so weird and how, and this was the biggie, he had got his nan to talk.

"Take-away again, then!" he said to himself. Chinese or Indian—it was the agony of choice. Not the chicken balls though—tasted like wadding. Or the vindaloo: not if he wanted to retain any portion of his sphincter intact. He chuckled to himself at the thought.

He went next to his bedroom, sat down on the unmade bed and looked around at the small box-like room. It was his, but it felt oppressive. Like a prison cell. His mum had worked hard to look after him and his nan since his dad had left, but money was tight and the small flat was all they could afford, especially in London . He hardly ever saw her.

She was out working different jobs at all hours and had left Joe since he was little to fend for himself. Every week saw her with a different boyfriend that she said would be "the one" to get them out of the mess they were in.

Then again, every week she'd say that the same boyfriend was a git and they were glad to be rid of him. It was almost laughable. It was laughable.

He threw himself back onto his bed.

The sound of whirring made him look up and he saw his hamster, Bernard, running on his wheel in his cage. The sight of the fat little form chugging away on the wheel always made him smile. The hamster had been a present a couple of years ago when

27

Mum had taken him down the Bingo and won some money. Joe had named the creature after the Bingo caller at the Bingo hall, who he had felt resembled the hamster. Even down to the teeth. Joe wondered idly what Bernard would look like in a bow tie.

"It has, Bernard, my little friend, been a very strange day. Do you want me to tell you about it?"

The whirring stopped, and Joe saw Bernard's backside wobble into a pile of chewed toilet roll and sawdust. The heap shook violently for a second, spouted sawdust, and then was still. Joe raised an eyebrow.

"You ignoring me as well? I thought at least you'd be up for listening. Ah, well."

Joe lay on the bed listening to the sound of the rain pattering on the window outside. He wished it would stop. It was interrupting his concentration. Names and places moved through his head and he only wished he had a computer to look them up. Then again, he also wished he could read. What he really wanted to do was to go back to the street where he had fainted and this time he would have a really good look around. Without the fainting part obviously.

Dorset Street. Dorset Street. And who was Mary Kelly? Before he knew it, Joe was asleep, his dreams full of crowded houses, squalid alleys and green eyes that glowed in the darkness…

CHAPTER THREE
IMAGES OF THE DEAD

Joe woke early that morning to the sound of the front door slamming and the voice of his mum calling his name. He was still fully dressed and his clothes were still slightly damp which made him shiver. Joe yawned and turned over, burying his head deep into his pillow. His mum's voice had the shrill and penetrating tone of a fire alarm. With another yawn and a muffled groan, Joe forced himself up out of bed and through the rubbish-strewn floor towards the sound of his mum's voice.

"What?" he grunted to his mum as he slouched into the sitting room. Nan was sitting exactly as before, and his mum was turning on the TV. Well, she was banging the top of it in the vain attempt to get it working.

Joe's mum was a short, rather pretty woman who had grown old before her time. She had had Joe as a teenager and, what with her own mother's catatonic state and her boyfriend walking out, had not had it easy. Despite this she always seemed cheerful and optimistic.

"Put the kettle on, love, and make us a cuppa. I'm knackered. God! It was hard work last night."

His mum ran her fingers through her hair, glancing in the mirror. She noticed that her roots were beginning to show through the dyed-at-home blonde she had put on it. *Grey*, she noticed with a rueful grin. She couldn't afford to have it done professionally at the hairdresser.

"What'd you get up to?" Joe called as he waded through the rubbish assault course to the kitchen, noticing with interest that the dead pot plant on the side had gained a green coating of mould like the one on the bathroom window.

"Never you mind!" came the reply.

It was always the same reply. Joe didn't like to think too much about it. Whatever she did, it kept a roof over their heads. He switched the kettle on and found a clean mug hiding behind a dirty one. "Mum," he dropped a tea bag into the cup, "ever heard of Dorset Street?"

The kettle boiled and clicked. Steam like old-fashioned smog filled the small room and made the dirty windows run with grime. Joe waited for a reply whilst filling the cup with water and a twice-used teabag. Nothing. He tried again.

"Mum…"

"I heard you!" The voice that came back sounded strained and tired. "Was once a street round the corner from here. Got demolished a while back. Not a nice place to be by all accounts. You made that tea yet?"

Joe could tell from the tone that it wouldn't be wise to press further—unless…

"Nan said it was the worst street in London".

He carried the tea into the living room and nearly spilt it as he almost bumped into his mum in the doorway. She seemed to fill the cramped space. Joe had never seen her so angry. Her hands were fists and her teeth were clenched. She looked like a cat on hot coals.

"Nan hasn't talked for over thirty years. What makes you think she'd remember a stupid street name?" Mum hissed at him.

Joe drew back, slopping hot tea over his hands but he was too frightened and startled to notice. He'd never seen his mum like this before, it was the same type of reaction that the people at the pub had about it all. Angry and sore. And yet through the anger he could sense something else from his mother.

Fear.

But not the fear he'd seen in her before when a boyfriend had punched or kicked her, or the landlord had threatened to evict them. This was an almost primal fear like that of an animal backed into a corner. The fear of something beyond comprehension. Something utterly evil and immoral.

"Sorry, Mum. I didn't mean to upset you. I was tired last night. Maybe I imagined it or heard it somewhere. Sorry." Joe held out the tea sheepishly and gave his mum what he thought was his best smile.

In an instant, his mum's face seemed to soften, and her body sagged. She looked old, worn and tired, like the flat.

"I'm sorry, too. I think I must be more tired than I thought." She ruffled Joe's hair and took the tea. "Thanks, love."

"I'll go out, Mum. Give you a rest. At least it's not raining today. You get some rest. There's a Bond film on later. You like a bit of Sean, or is it Roger?"

"Cheeky!" His mum swatted at him and took the cup to the sofa where she sat down and put her feet up on a ragged orange stool. Joe could see that she was calmer now but could see her eyes flitting furtively over to Nan. Without another word, Joe put on his coat and left the flat.

***

The boy stood at the entrance to the service road and looked at the car park squatting like a living creature at the end of it. It was still deserted and forlorn. Everywhere Joe looked was rubbish and litter. Weeds pushed themselves up through the broken concrete in a pathetic attempt to reach what there was of the sun. Puddles full of last night's rain had crisp packets and fast food wrappers sailing in their murky waters, like little boats.

The sound of traffic along Commercial Road behind him seemed faint and distant as if in a different time, a different world. Even though the sun was shining, it never seemed to fall on the little side street, as if it were afraid to settle there. Shadows crept everywhere. If Joe had believed in ghosts, they'd be here.

Joe stared hard and tried to visualise what he had seen before. Nothing happened, nothing at all. No movement, no change of image. He even tried waggling his eyebrows. Joe was just beginning to wonder if he had imagined it all, maybe he'd just been feeling unwell from getting so wet in the rain, when out of the corner of his eye he saw it. He swallowed hard, remembering the words of the strange man from the pub.

"There are things about this city, this world, boy, that you can never imagine…"

Like a dim image that seemed to swim out of the air, like a picture from an old silent movie, something came into view. The image was jerky and uncoordinated as if it was struggling to enter Joe's world. Air rippled as if in a heat haze, but there was no heat, only an intense cold. The cold of the grave, the cold of death.

Somewhere, on the wind, a bell was ringing…

A young woman seemed to materialise out of the air, dressed in clothes of a bygone age. She couldn't have been much older than twenty-five. Her dress, which would once have been red, was splashed with mud and patched. She wore a dirty, black shawl over her shoulders and held a small wicker basket that contained what looked like violets. The woman then looked directly at him. Her face was pretty but careworn and Joe was reminded at once of his mother. Her hair was drawn back in a bun, but some spilled out around her face like sea grass moving underwater. But it was her eyes that drew his attention. Deep and black like someone else he knew. In them seemed to be reflected all the sorrow and pity of living in such a place. The vision held out her hand and Joe felt his arm jerk involuntarily towards her.

And then she smiled at him.

Joe jumped as a hand grabbed his shoulder. He spun round to see Flo Kelly, startled by his movement, taking a step backwards in alarm and almost falling into one of the grubby puddles. By the time he looked back, the woman was gone.

Within the prison of stone, the entity shifted uneasily. This was not part of the plan. The woman had no right to interfere, although soon it knew the interference from that quarter would soon cease. But it was interference no less. In frustration, it bellowed into the blackness that surrounded it. The woman would pay, and it knew just how to do it. The boy, however, the boy was different and not of his time.

Someone else had started playing the Game.

Suddenly the darkness deepened as the prisoner in stone gently probed the mind of the boy. The darkness flashed with something that looked like green eyes before becoming absolute. The prisoner gained new knowledge. The boy was...necessary.

Joe went wild. "The woman! Did you see her? The woman in the dress! You must have seen her! No one wears clothes like that anymore!"

Flo was even more startled than she had been before and held up her hands in alarm. "Whoa! Calm down, Joe. I didn't see anyone. No one was there. I just wanted to say sorry for yesterday. I took it too far and I'm sorry. It was stupid of me. I didn't think, that's all. I say stuff before my brain has a chance to process...Joe? Are you listening?"

She saw that Joe was staring ahead at an empty space in the car park covered by shadow that, as she blinked, seemed to crawl away. She blinked again and the moment was gone. Dismissing the sight from her mind for the moment, Flo waved her hand in front of Joe's face. She felt quite relieved when he turned to her.

"Sorry? What did you say?" His voice was hoarse, and Flo wasn't sure if it was shaking slightly. Whatever Joe had seen, it had appeared real to him. Flo tried again.

"I said I'm sorry. For yesterday." The teenager shuffled awkwardly. It hurt her to admit that she was wrong. "Edward said you had issues. I didn't know." Flo scraped the floor with her foot, dirtying the top of her purple trainer with puddle muck. "I wanted to apologise. I saw you leaving your flat so I followed you here."

"Right." Joe turned back to look at the shadowy car park. Flo was sure the boy hadn't even heard what she had said. "Are you sure you didn't see her? The woman in the red dress and black shawl? Flowers in a basket."

Flo shrugged. "Maybe she went into the car park. I don't know." She pointed to a shadowy opening in the wall of the car

34

park that looked like the entrance to a ghost train. "That's the only way out of the car park, there."

"Come on!" Flo was surprised, and almost stumbled, as Joe grabbed her hand and started running towards the car park at full pelt.

"Hey! What are you doing, you moron!" Flo struggled but felt as if she needed to humour him.

They both ran across the street, towards the opening Flo had pointed to that now loomed large before them like the mouth of some long extinct creature.

***

It was dark in the entrance to the car park. There were only a few old, cheap cars parked in it and both Joe and Flo could see why. The whitewashed walls were stained with graffiti and dirt. Black, stagnant puddles on the filthy concrete floor were fed by the constant dripping of water that bled from the ceiling. Crime and squalor seemed embedded in the very fabric of the building. Any decent car would have been jacked long before now.

It was also very empty.

"Hello?" Joe called into the smothering gloom. "You there?" His voice echoed weirdly around the empty space, bouncing off the walls and into nothing.

There was no reply except the sound of dripping water, while the wind whistled and echoed through the desolate structure. A filthy cobweb blew in the wind. They moved through the low doorway.

Together the two teenagers searched every inch of the building. There was no one there. It was deserted. Joe slumped on a low wall and ran a hand through his hair. He let out a loud sigh and looked up at Flo who plonked herself down next to him and smoothed down the creases on her black velvet mini skirt.

"I suppose you think I made it up to get back at you?" Joe muttered glumly.

"No." The answer surprised him. "I feel something in here. Something old, so old and unable to rest. It's if the whole place is full of ghosts and memories crowding out from the shadows. I thought I saw something myself when I met you here." The girl shivered as the memory of the crawling shadow came back to her. "Silly, really." Flo shrugged and shifted on her seat uncomfortably.

"So, you believe me? That I saw the woman?"

"Yes. It was the look on your face that said it all. Have you seen anything like this before?" Flo looked earnestly at Joe waiting for an answer. She had always had an interest in the supernatural and wasn't called "goth girl" at school for no good reason. Probably why she had so few friends. Or maybe it had something to do with the black makeup and multiple piercings that the school rules didn't allow.

Joe hesitated then looked again at Flo. He was impressed that she had believed him, but then he didn't want to give her any more ammunition for school. Not that it mattered anyway. The fact they all thought he was thick was ammunition enough.

"Last night...after I left you...I was angry. I walked to that bus stop over there. I didn't know where I was. I couldn't read the bus sign properly...mostly because I'm a meat head and can't read." He shot a look at Flo who had the good grace to blush and turn away. "Anyway, I went to cross the road, to that pub there, when some stupid car nearly knocked me over and I ended up at the edge of this service road."

Joe paused. He looked at Flo who nodded briefly in encouragement, took a deep breath and carried on.

"I then…it was strange, as if the whole place was spinning. The air was shimmering and stuff and then…the car park. It changed. I can't explain it really. It…it became a proper street, all broken down like. More mucked up than this place is now. It seemed alive…Flo?"

Joe noticed that Flo was no longer looking at him. Her gaze was riveted to a dirty puddle a few feet from them. Her eyes were like dinner plates. Joe looked at the puddle. Floating in it was a sprig of violet, spinning as if recently dropped. Flo spoke, her voice a whisper.

"I know what this place was. I've read about it in books. Dorset Street. The worst street in London." She turned and ran. Joe took a final look at the piece of spinning violet and ran after her.

***

Joe and Flo didn't stop running until they had put some distance between them and the car park. They threw themselves down on a patch of waste ground and got their breath back. Joe turned to Flo.

"Why'd you hightail it out of there like that for? You mad or something?" He couldn't help grinning at her despite the strange turn of events.

He felt a sharp smack to the head as Flo cuffed him round the ear. Joe turned still grinning, but the smile was wiped from his face when he saw how pale the girl's face was. *Suits the makeup*, Joe thought. Then the words came out of Flo in a torrent.

"God! You really have no idea, have you? About what that place was? Dorset Street…you really don't listen in history lessons, do you? Maybe I was right about you being thick. If you had been listening to anything old Lusky boy was saying about the East End, you'd know that Dorset Street was famous for crime and poverty. It makes our East End seem like a paradise compared to what those poor people had to go through.

"Some houses had three families in one small room. Absolutely filthy and so lawless even the police wouldn't go there except in twos and threes, if at all." She breathed heavily and swallowed hard to lubricate her suddenly dry mouth.

"Oh." Joe stared back the way they had just come. He thought back to what the man in the pub and his nan had said. His words came out softly and gently. "I knew that. My nan used that exact same phrase last night. Dorset Street: The worst street in London."

He then snapped out of his reverie. "So, what? Why'd you move so fast? You ain't the one seeing things apart from a stupid shadow, so what got you so spooked?" He felt confused but also relieved that he seemed to now have someone who really did believe in what he had seen.

"You described the place and didn't even know what it was or where it was, and then the flowers floating in the water. How did you know?'

"Coincidence?" Joe replied but knew he wasn't convincing himself. He could hear it himself in his voice.

"You really don't know what happened there, do you? What that place is really famous for?" Flo was incredulous.

38

"No." Even though he had no idea what Flo was going to say, Joe knew that whatever it was, it was bad. Bad enough for a tough, not caring-a-toss girl like Flo to run as if she was being chased by the devil himself. With what she said next, thought Joe, she may well have been.

"Jack. Jack the Ripper," Flo whispered.

CHAPTER FOUR
THE MYSTERY DEEPENS

Joe took a deep breath. Despite his lack of interest in history and lessons in general, even he had heard of Jack the Ripper. But that had happened over one hundred years ago, deep in the murky history of Victorian London. So why was he seeing images from a past long since dead and buried under the trappings of a modern city? It just didn't make sense. Unless...unless of course he was mad. Joe shook his head to dismiss the thought.

"So, what you're saying..." he began.

"Is that you are seeing images of this service road and car park when they were Dorset Street." interrupted Flo. "I know that you aren't making it up as you would have had no idea what this place was or what the people there would have been wearing at the time." She sounded so superior.

Joe smiled despite himself. "You're saying I'm too much of a moron to be lying, aren't you?"

"Yes...no. I just want to know why you've started to see these things and what we're going to do about it."

"You can't tell anyone," Joe said desperately to Flo. "They all think I'm strange at school as it is. Even stranger than you. I don't want them taking me away from home like some kind of nut..." He faltered. He was intrigued and scared about it all at the same time. "Just...just don't tell anyone, okay?"

Flo looked at Joe with interest. She'd never looked at him properly before. He was the boy from a broken home that no one rated. She narrowed her eyes as if seeing him properly for the first time. A tall boy with lean limbs and a shock of dark hair looked back at her. He was thin; Flo thought she'd never seen anyone quite as thin before. His face was even thinner, angular, making his brown eyes appear even larger. Joe had a hungry look about him, not starving exactly, but hungry.

"I think better with a full stomach. You eaten today?" She watched him shake his head. "Come on, then. There's a café round the corner. I'll buy you a bun."

Joe realised himself that he was hungry. He hadn't eaten properly since school yesterday. The wind whistled down the street and tugged at his clothes, the same damp clothes he'd been wearing the day before, Joe thought with embarrassment. He realised that he was also cold, that it wasn't just down to the weather. Joe shrugged his shoulders in agreement and the two of them made their way down the main road towards the café.

***

The café was agreeably warm, in a shabby kind of way much like the clientele. The windows were steamed and murky, the atmosphere grubby and smelling of grease and fried food. It made Joe feel even hungrier than before. He munched on his bun, savouring the sweet, chewy texture and the crunchy sugar granules scattered liberally on the top.

Flo watched Joe eat and wondered when he had a square meal. "What is happening to you?" she said at last. Joe shook his

41

head and shrugged his shoulders and mumbled incoherently through the crumbs.

"That woman you saw." Flo tried again, pushing another bun towards him. "Do you think you may have seen her picture in a book, somewhere or on the telly?"

Joe shook his head, swallowed the last of the bun and started working on the second. "No. I've never seen her before. I'd remember her if I did. I've never seen a face so sad and full of unhappiness. And the clothes would be a dead giveaway. No one wears stuff like that nowadays. Not unless you are a nutter or something," he added pointedly at Flo, eyeing her black, gothic outfit.

"I think we should have a look through the books in the library," Flo was saying, ignoring Joe's look. "We might see if we can find a picture of her or someone like her in the history section."

Joe groaned and slumped his head forward onto the chipped melamine table before sliding despondently to the floor. He looked imploringly up at Flo who stared down at him with a wry smile on her face. "Not books. I don't do books…"

"Then look at the pictures!" Flo snapped. She felt annoyed but tried to remember what it must be like for Joe not to be able to read. "Sorry, that was unfair. Look, I'll help you. Joe? Oi! Joe, are you listening to me?"

Joe wasn't looking at her anymore. He seemed to be staring right past her and his mouth hung open. Flo followed his gaze noticing the look of astonishment on his face. Joe was staring at an old drawing on the wall of the café. It was of a woman in her late twenties.

A sad smile seemed to play on her lips. Flo thought she could hear the sound of a bell ringing, far away, as if on the wind. Except they were inside a café and there was no wind.

"That's her." Joe whispered. "That's the woman, I saw."

Flo squinted until she could read the caption under the picture. It was a name with a surname that matched her own.

"Mary Kelly," squeaked Flo.

CHAPTER FIVE
EDDOWS

Edward Eddows was a smart boy. He was what the teachers would call a model pupil and what the other pupils would call "posh." That, he had always thought ruefully to himself, was probably due to his parents' ridiculous idea that a name that was alliterative was a good idea. That said, to all at school Edward was reliable, clever, acid-tongued and sharp when roused, good-looking to the point of ludicrous and never in trouble.

He was also trustworthy which is why Edward (or Eddows as he preferred to be called) had sat quietly and calmly through the gabbled story told to him by Joe and Flo. He sat quietly because he didn't trust himself to answer in a sensible way. He could feel the mounting confusion and excitement inside him and the quickening of his heart. Eddows also felt they could be pulling his leg.

"Let me get this right." His voice betrayed no trace of the wonder that he felt as he rubbed his hands over his eyes. "You've been seeing past events and your nan, Joe, who hasn't spoken in over thirty years, has now started talking?"

"Well, yes. And there was this strange man in the pub." Joe replied, although now that both he and Flo were sat in the school library surrounded by lots of other children, teachers, the very handsome, very rational Eddows and the trappings of the 21st century, he began to wonder if both he and Flo had either imagined it, or had been acting out what they thought was real in some kind of bizarre fantasy.

"Well, most pubs contain some kind of strange, drunk-as-a-skunk clientele, so we don't have to worry much about that."

Eddows stood up decisively and put his hands together and clicked his fingers loudly, enjoying the wincing look on the other two faces at the startling cracking noise.

"We'd better get started then. Find out all we can about this Dorset Street and what happened to Mary Kelly. I suggest we go to the history section first or we go and look at the public records. They may be able to tell us more. What do you think?"

Flo and Joe stared open mouthed at Eddows. "You mean that you believe us?' Flo managed to stammer. "Everything we've said, and you don't think we're mad?"

Eddows smoothed down his immaculate clothing, smiled condescendingly at them and brushed a stray blond hair from his collar. "Of course, I believe you, although it is true that you are both obviously stark raving mad. But I don't think either of you have the imagination to come up with something like that—even with your combined brain cells. I exaggerate. You might be lucky if you were rubbing the one between you."

He strode calmly towards the bookshelves leaving the two startled mullets behind him.

"What about my seeing things and stuff?" an astonished Joe managed to mutter after him.

"One thing at a time!" came the measured response as Eddows vanished behind the nearest pile of books.

"If we find out some hard facts about people and places, we might be able to work out what is happening to you. I suggest we start with the year of the Jack the Ripper murders...1888, I

45

believe. I'm pulling what we call books, things that hold knowledge, Joe, off the shelf."

Eddows' head appeared round the side of the shelf.

"Just in case you were thinking I was doing witchcraft or something."

The head disappeared with a derisive snort as Joe threw a rubber at it.

There was a pause and the sound of more volumes being pulled from the shelves. Then, "I admit that I find that you, Joe, the most interesting thing about all of this, what with you seeing visions but, and this is the thing, if we go in armed, so to speak, with some prior knowledge of what is happening to you, then we might be able to solve everything. Flo, unfortunately I am sure I won't be able to help you. You are just mad."

"So what do you intend to do, oh Jedi Master?"

Flo was becoming infuriated with the unflappable Eddows and his so superior attitude. What was also bothering her was that she felt quite attracted to his unflappability, and how could anyone be that good-looking? And Eddows? He didn't even seem to have batted an eyelid about the events.

"I'm not sure yet!" came the infuriatingly cheerful reply of Edward Eddows from behind the pile of books. An arm holding a heavy tome shot out in front of the surprised girl.

"Here, hold this one."

***

It was a miserable and disillusioned threesome that finally sat back, or in Joe's case, assumed his usual position with his head slumped on the desk in front of him on the library chairs at the end of the day. They had spent the last three hours going through every book on the Victorian East End that they could find, and beyond the standard stuff of the appalling poverty the residents of Dorset Street had to suffer and the terrible murder of Mary Kelly by Jack the Ripper, there was nothing of any note. Every book told the same gruesome story in a slightly different way.

"Stuff this! This is stupid! What a waste of time!" Joe had found the whole process tedious in the extreme, even more so as he couldn't read any of the books that Eddows had put in front of him.

"There was nothing much different on the computer searches, either. Well, none of the websites the school will let us on," Flo said gazing out of the library window at the gathering black clouds.

Pulling himself up, Joe picked up half a dozen of the books and proceeded to stuff them back onto the shelves in random order. In his mood he couldn't have cared less if the books had split or torn, but for Eddows that was another matter. He leapt to his feet and tried to stop Joe's trail of destruction. Joe was so cross that he started to push Eddows away; Flo seeing the danger, tried to intervene and all three ended up in a heap on the floor as books rained heavily down upon their heads.

"Joe, you really are a complete and utter moronic sap!" Eddows snarled crossly at the boy.

But Joe wasn't listening.

He was clutching his head and shaking it hard, his teeth gritted in pain. Then to Eddows and Flo's horror, Joe threw himself backwards across the room and began to crawl towards the door. Eddows was just thankful that the library was empty at this time of the day.

"Joe! Joe! What's wrong?" Flo cried out, her voice becoming a scream as Joe lurched to his feet and flung himself through the doors to the corridor outside, his body crashing against the wall as if flung by some kind of invisible force.

"It won't stop! The voices inside my head! Screaming…so much pain! So much pain and fear! It's happened again! I can feel… death! I can feel it! Burning in my brain! I've got to go back! Find out if…" Joe's voice reverberated again and again from down the corridor.

Flo shot a look at Eddows and shouted, "Move! After him!" They both crashed through the library doors after him.

The darkness shifted and gloated to itself. Another Contract had been destroyed. Snuffed out like the flame from a flickering candle. No one would miss her though, down among the slime of the filthy streets. No one but her few remaining friends and their numbers grew small. In the pitch black of its stone prison it shifted again and thought that its idea of making the boy experience some of the pain of its last victim had been an exceptional idea. Probing the boy's mind had been simple. Child's play. The Game had begun. And there were now two new players…

***

"Where's he going? What's wrong with him?" panted Eddows as he and Flo raced down the street. In front of them they could just see the reeling figure of Joe disappearing into the gathering twilight.

Rain had begun to fall again, adding to the puddles of the previous day and the pair of them found themselves splashing through the dirty water.

"He's going to the car park—the service road!" gasped Flo. "The site of Dorset Street!" The pair of them rounded the corner that led to the car park, just as the sound of a bell pealed through the driving rain so loudly and with such force that both teens were flung off their feet to land battered and bruised on the ground.

When they looked up, Joe had gone.

CHAPTER SIX
INTO DARKNESS

Joe reached the site of Dorset Street only moments before the others. The voices in his head cried out to him, driving him onwards. They were muddled and distorted and he couldn't work out what they were saying to him.

He felt that if he reached the car park then they might stop. Joe didn't notice the gathering gloom or the pouring rain. He heard the sound of the bell, but it was louder this time. So loud that the force of the sound had knocked him to the ground: Ground that shifted under him and then seemed to melt beneath him.

Joe felt himself falling. The darkness pressed in around him as if trying to smother him in velvet blackness. He felt sick. His head felt like it was being squeezed in a vice and it would explode at any moment. Joe closed his eyes and felt and heard a rushing sound. A bitterly cold wind had begun to blow, and it was at that moment he felt that he was drowning. That he couldn't breathe. And then, suddenly Joe realised that he was wet. Soaking wet as if being battered by a monsoon. The sound of the wind increased to a roar; Joe had never heard a noise so terrifying before. It cut through the teeming voices in his head, silencing them instantly with its own screaming.

Joe felt his body hit the floor.

He lay there for a long time with his eyes tightly shut. The sound of the wind died away until it became nothing more than an icy breeze over his prone body. The wetness had reduced to the gentle pattering of rain in puddles. Joe felt stiff and cold all over. He moved slightly and winced with the effort. "I'm starting to make a habit of this," the boy murmured to himself through dry lips. He slowly opened his eyes and saw that he had landed in a puddle. He thought at first that it was the same puddle he had splashed through by the service road until he realised that houses were crowding in on him on all sides. Dark, narrow houses lit by the dull glow of gas and candlelight. Joe slowly, and with some difficulty, sat up and looked around.

The scene was one he had seen before. The image of the street that had come out of the car park, but this time, this time he was in it. Joe was sitting in the street of his vision. Along with the crowded, higgledy-piggledy houses, he could see battered gas lights that ranged along the street, steep steps that led down into black cellars and underground rooms, weeds that were growing on the sides of the street and rubbish stuck like wet paper in the deep pools and hollows that pitted the road. The smell was appalling: a mixture of stale meat, mould and rotting vegetables and something else...

Joe wrinkled his nose and gagged. It was worse than the smell when he had that dodgy curry from the Indian take-away that had been closed down due to a health and safety check and it had felt like his insides had run out. He looked around to see if there were any blocked drains and then realised that there were none. The street was deep in filth. Joe thought his eyes were playing tricks on him. The filth seemed to move, and then to his horror, a big black rat scuttled forth from under the mire and

51

across the street, followed by another and another until Joe felt his skin begin to crawl. He was too stunned to move but knew he couldn't sit where he was for much longer. He also couldn't believe that anyone could live in this pit and yet he knew from what the other two had told him that there could be anything up to thirty people in one room.

The place was a living hell.

***

Flo and Eddows picked themselves up from the ground and stared. The service road was empty, and the car park locked. There was nowhere for Joe to have gone. The rain bounced dully off the parked cars and bollards. The darkness that had been gathering was now complete and the pair strained their eyes into the gloom, taking in every corner of the road. Nothing. Joe had completely disappeared.

"I'm not sure that I have any answers for this," Eddows whispered as he dusted himself down and adjusted his crumpled top. Flo smiled in spite of herself. She was taking rather a liking to this Eddows who knew naff all. It made him more human. It was then that she noticed something floating, sodden in a puddle.

Flo bent down and picked it out from amongst the muddy, dirty water. It was a small sprig of violet. Suddenly, from the darkness, came the sound of tinkling laughter. Both Flo and Eddows whirled round in the direction of the sound and saw what appeared to be the dark hem of a red petticoat, splattered with mud, vanishing into the pedestrian entrance of the car park.

Without thinking, they ran towards the shape and went crashing into the locked gate. Peering through the mesh grill they saw the form of a woman gliding into the darkness beyond. As she moved deeper into the car park the light from the emergency exit sign fell in a ghostly, sickly green glow across her back, revealing knotted blonde hair falling over the grubby black shawl.

"It's her…" Flo whispered. "It's really her. Mary Kelly. The last victim of the Ripper. What to do? Can we talk to her?"

Eddows just shook his head. For once he wasn't sure what to do and the feeling bothered him somewhat.

"I don't know. Is she really there?"

"What do you mean?" Flo glanced at Eddows, his face white and drawn. "What do you mean, 'is she really there?' You can see her, can't you?"

Eddows swallowed hard. "Some people believe that certain buildings and places that are said to be haunted are like radio receivers. That they have energy from the past imprinted in their very fabric that is replayed again and again, like a memory. We might be experiencing that memory now. That is the rational explanation."

"And the irrational?"

"That she's a ghost and you could always try talking to her. But I don't believe it. I can't believe it."

"Mary! Mary Kelly!"

Flo was surprised to find the name had come from her own throat. The young woman ahead of them stopped. Flo's namesake slowly turned and looked at them, a mocking smile on her lips and the dark shawl she wore around her shoulders moved as if by some invisible force. She put a finger to her lips.

The rusty bolts of the gate Eddows and Flo were leaning on shot open as if by magic and they fell into the car park.

They looked up to see the shape of the woman beckoning them to follow into the shadows. The wind moaned through the car park and the woman's hair seemed to float around her face like wreaths of smoke. Her eyes, however, were like black holes, as bottomless as the pits of Hades.

As if in a dream Flo went to follow her, but Eddows held her back. "Look at her!" He whispered through clenched teeth and Flo could feel him shaking beside her. "Look at her! Don't you see? She's a shadow of the past. It can't be real. It can't!"

Eddows' ever-analytical mind was struggling to comprehend what was going on and finding it was no good. How could this be happening? This was not rational. *This*, thought Eddows, *does not compute*. "This is not real," he whispered again.

Flo was angry now. She wanted to know what had happened to Joe. "Then tell me just why you and I can see the same thing then, if it—she is dead! She looks real enough to me!"

The woman in the shadows beckoned them again. Grabbing Eddows firmly by the arm, and with more confidence than she felt, Flo stepped towards the apparition. The ghostly green light seemed to intensify as they neared the shape; it surrounded them and became brighter. Still the shape beckoned them nearer until Flo felt she could reach out and touch her. The light grew brighter still and Eddows felt his eyes water. Flo's hand shot forward and grabbed the wrist of the thing that wore the shape of Mary Kelly and felt cold and…bone?

The ghost of the past looked up and stared Flo full in the face and in the pits of the dead reflected there, the girl saw such sorrow and hardship her heart lurched in her chest and filled with pity. The temperature dropped rapidly, causing both of them to shiver, and then everything went black.

Flo and Eddows were alone in the car park. On the floor, in the puddle, under the now quite normal emergency light, floated petals of violets.

***

Joe slumped against a dripping post. He was tired and cold and wet. Again. He had walked up and down the street debating whether or not to knock on any of the doors. He then thought better of it. He imagined how he would feel opening the door to some stranger, wearing weird clothes late at night, in the pouring rain. Joe swore under his breath and smacked the lamppost in frustration. It hurt, which actually felt good. At least it felt real. What the hell was he going to do? He had no idea where he was.

It then hit him. He did know where he was! Just because the place looked different, didn't mean that it wasn't the same piece of land he had been standing on over one hundred years in the future! If he walked towards that lamp post he'd find himself on the main street and if he were right, then there would be a pub called the Ten Bells at the end of it. Some of the buildings must still exist. At least he hoped they did. Feeling in a much more positive frame of mind, Joe headed off in the direction of the main street, and the pub.

In the darkness, it began to rejoice. The main pawn in the new Game had arrived to watch the visions of the past unfold…

***

Flo and Eddows sat on the low wall next to the car park. Flo held the violet petals in her hands. They felt of ice and of the grave. She felt terrible—if only she hadn't touched the woman then maybe they would have found Joe. If only she hadn't been so impulsive—or stupid.

"Why'd you have to be so stupid?" muttered Eddows under his breath. He turned away from Flo, his handsome face crumpled like a piece of paper, his blue eyes clouded with uncertainty. It was the first time that Flo had ever seen him confused and upset. Normally he was just so unflappable. What had happened in the car park had obviously shaken him a great deal. But then again, what they had both experienced would shake anyone. When Eddows spoke again, it was slowly and with feeling.

"I don't believe in ghosts, phantoms or ghouls. Or things that go bump in the night. How can you in this day and age? You know, with computers, the Internet, mobile phones and all the other things. It's just…mad. Insane. I can't…and yet there it, she, was just standing there in front of us: this woman thing from the past who was the last victim of a serial killer. I might as well believe in the tooth fairy and before you say it, Flo, I didn't get given an obscene amount of money for each tooth. Well, no more than I deserved. Oh…"

Eddows stood up and angrily kicked the nearest bollard. He started to hop about holding his foot, swearing loudly. Flo tried not to laugh but hysteria got the better of her and she began to shake with laughter. Eddows stared at her and then the moment got him too and the pair collapsed against the wall.

Eventually, all laughter spent, they sat up. Flo let out a deep breath and turned to Eddows.

"Joe. We're going to get him back."

***

Joe stood outside the Ten Bells Public House. Apart from a different sign, the outside of the pub looked virtually identical to its modern-day equivalent. Still grubby and still with peeling paint decking the outside. Inside, Joe could hear the sound of raised voices and loud, tuneless singing.

He watched as the doors to the pub flew open and a dirty-looking man was flung onto the street. The man spun on his bottom and came to rest close to Joe. He staggered to his feet and Joe could see that the man was drunk.

The eyes didn't focus and instead looked straight through him. The man started singing in a loud, cracked voice, heaved himself to his feet, and reeled off up the street. Taking a deep breath, if that was to be the type of people who frequented the pub, Joe took a firm grip of the handle, and stepped inside.

CHAPTER SEVEN
MURDER!

The pub had hardly changed in the one hundred odd years since Joe had been there last, with the exception that it was crowded with people. Young and old, men and women: all crowded in together like filthy rats in a trap. Not one of them was smartly dressed. They all appeared to be wearing clothes that had seen better days. The nearest man had an old threadbare jacket patched and discoloured with age. The women were not much better, with ragged dresses and petticoats with motheaten shawls slung over their shoulders. What really caught Joe's attention was the fact that many of the women were smoking small clay pipes.

When he looked again, some of the children who were sitting at the foot of the bar were also smoking and drinking. *Mr Lusk would have a field day*, he thought. The smell of smoke and cheap booze filled his nostrils and thick, almost greasy smog hung over the place. Despite the strangeness of the situation, Joe couldn't help but smile at the sight. It all seemed so absurd.

No one noticed him as he wormed his way through the bar. Joe saw that some of the paintings on the wall were the same as in the present day. He recognised the street from a painting showing it in more salubrious times. In another, men and women were working at looms and the place seemed to have a more prosperous air that had long since passed. Joe found a corner by the side of one of the battered chairs that were strewn across the pub and settled down. It may have been dirty, smelly and noisy but it was at least dry and warm.

In fact, Joe was beginning to feel decidedly hot. He took off his jacket and covered himself up with it. He hadn't realised just how tired he was, and his eyes were just closing despite the clamour when the door of the pub was slammed inwards and the same man that Joe had seen leave staggered in.

He wasn't singing now.

His eyes had found their focus and were wide with terror. The man's face was red and swollen and his mouth was opening and shutting like a goldfish. The ragged clientele of the pub turned to him. One word managed to issue forth from his gulping lips.

"Murder!"

In an instant the pub was in an uproar. Joe was by now very much awake and he pulled himself to a crouching position, down by the side of the chair. The man had turned out through the door once more, followed by most of the pub.

Joe could feel the fear running through the night air like icy fingers that plucked at the people within. The women threw each other worried glances and some of the more bullish-looking men took up their beer bottles like weapons and strode out of the pub. Without waiting, Joe slipped out through the side door and followed the men at a safe distance down the street.

From his position at the back of the mob, Joe could hear the drunken man repeating his mantra, "Murder!" over and over again, his voice becoming higher and more hysterical. Some of the leading men had now lit torches, which flung greasy, blue flames into the wet and murky air.

The mob marched down dark and winding alleys, through dank and disused courts, until they arrived at a dismal yard at the back of another road that Joe could just about read, named Berner Street. Joe took a hard look at the mob. They consisted of the usual crowd of hysterical woman decked out in poorly made clothes, some small rough-looking children who should have been in bed and a young man with lank hair. Joe could see another man remonstrating with the drunk and take him roughly to one side.

In the distance, he could hear the shrill sound of a police whistle. Weaving his way through the crowd, Joe crawled between the legs of the men at the front, so he could get a look at what the others could see.

From the stones, it felt nothing but grim satisfaction. The vessel had done the job well, performed the task with, if not precision, competency. Another annoyance gone to meet her maker in the vilest way possible. Another Contract terminated. If only it had the means to move further abroad instead of being trapped within its surroundings. Finding the vessel again had been a bonus but drained its power greatly, forcing it to return to the prison it had frequented for so long… still, it had been enough.

The sight made Joe stop dead where he was standing. On the ground lay a woman. She wasn't young, and she wasn't old. She must have been around the same age as his mother and that was what was so terrible.

This woman could have been his mother.

The only comforting thought was that his mother was over one hundred years in the future. She lay at a slight angle as if she had been laid down to sleep on the dirty ground.

But Joe knew that the woman on the ground wasn't asleep. She would never wake again.

A commotion at the back of the mob shook the horrified and stunned Joe from his reverie, and he turned to see a short man leading a policeman towards the body. He then noticed that some of the onlookers were staring at him strangely and muttering to themselves. Joe felt his stomach lurch—maybe they thought he did it. That he had killed the woman. He moved himself away from the body on the ground.

"Here! Here she is!" cried the man and Joe detected the trace of an accent in the man's trembling voice. He'd heard it before somewhere, in an old war movie he had seen one day when he'd been off school sick. Was it Jewish?

Joe watched as the policeman knelt down by the body and slowly lifted up the head. He could see quite clearly a dark pool staining the cobbles beneath and turned away in shock. He stumbled away to the entrance of the yard and was violently sick against the wall. Joe laid his head against the rough brick, closed his eyes and was glad of the dampness for once. A cold breeze ruffled his hair and cooled his burning forehead. When he turned back, most of the crowd had dispersed with the policeman to find a doctor or physician.

Joe noticed that the youngish man with the lank hair was also being sick against the nearest wall, and what looked like a pool of bile had collected on the ground. *Odd colour*, Joe thought. *Blue*.

Through his own tearful eyes, the bile appeared to him to move and climb the walls as if it were alive, mixing and mingling with the shadows that crowded in on the small yard. Joe shook his head and the odd vision disappeared along with the man who

61

seemed to melt away into the darkness. Only the small Jewish man remained crouched by the corpse, almost tenderly cradling her head.

"Did you know her?" Joe stepped towards the man. The man didn't respond.

"I said, did you know her?" he repeated louder this time. He felt some respect had to be shown to the woman, whoever she was. Still nothing. Joe looked at the man. He appeared frozen and unmoving, like a puppet with its strings cut. Joe went up to the man and waved his hand over the man's eyes. They appeared as dead and still as the woman at his feet.

"He won't talk."

Words hissed from the darkness, cutting the air like knives. Joe whirled round and strained his eyes into the smog and darkness. "He won't talk. None of them will."

"Where…who are you?" Joe called out to the bitter air, watching his breath becoming one with the smog. The darkness in front of him seemed to grow even thicker, swelling and forming shapes that mimicked the shadows thrown out by the wan lamplight from the surrounding houses. They crawled and raced across the broken cobbles and stopped near Joe, surrounding him, circling him, like lapping waves in a dead sea. Mocking laughter echoed and bounced off the shattered walls and buildings, filling Joe's head until he felt it would burst.

"Who are you?" Joe shouted, and he swore that just for a moment, from the empty blackness before him, a shape of a face with cold, cruel, inhuman eyes and jutting horns smiled at him before fading away into the darkness.

"So many questions in one so young. Never you mind. I am what I am. You'll be seeing me again, child," grated the inhuman

62

sound. "I just wanted you to know I am here and watching. And waiting."

The darkness swirled up and around him like mist. It pulled and tugged at his clothes and then the blackness swallowed him up. And then came the pressure. Joe had never felt pressure like it.

He had never been diving before, but he had heard that divers suffered from what was called "the bends," a squeezing of internal organs causing immense pain. He had never had the bends, but if he had, this is what it must feel like. Joe felt his knees buckle and give way; such was the pain.

And now you know, child, what I can do, it thought to itself. *Just a little display of what I can do. Just one little rip...*

And then it was gone.

The boy knew then where and more importantly *when* he was. The year was 1888. The year that the East End of London descended into fear. The year that the East End would witness the most brutal and mysterious murders in all of its long history.

Joe slumped, stunned, bruised and terrified in the ever-present darkness as the wind tore through the yard and the gasping gas candles were extinguished one by one as cries of "Ripper! Ripper!" echoed through the night.

***

Eddows and Flo stood in the entrance to the car park. A stiff breeze made them both shiver. Flo pulled up her coat collar and swung her arms around herself to keep warm. The pair of them had been waiting for hours, but for what they didn't know.

63

Eddows gave a loud yawn, which prompted a sharp nudge in the ribs from Flo.

"Stay awake, for crying out loud. And stop yawning like that, showing off those perfect teeth. No one should look as perfect as you! I said stop yawning. You'll set me off!"

"Sorry. It's just we've been here all night and bugger all has happened. And my teeth are part of my beauty regime. I plan on staying as young looking as I can. You should give it a go instead of all that gothic makeup caking your face. You look like a clown."

"Stuff you," came the terse reply followed by another sharp dig into Eddows' ribs. "I'm cold. Wish I'd worn my scarf."

"Wish I was in bed."

Eddows winced and stretched and rubbed his tired eyes, cross he'd not remembered to moisturise before he'd come. He couldn't remember a time when he'd felt so tired. Yawning again, he pushed the palms of his hands into his eyes and a multitude of bright colours welled up into his sockets. He released the pressure and the colours burst outwards and away, seeming to dance before his vision, but unlike they usually did, they didn't fade away.

They continued to dance and swirl but then he noticed only in one particular spot in front of him—he looked at Flo and he could see that she was just as transfixed by the colours. They seemed to pull in on themselves like water swirling down a plughole.

"This is it!" shrieked Flo, her face determined, a mixture of excitement and fear.

"This is it!" she cried again whilst grabbing Eddows' arm hard, making him wince in pain as her nails gripped his skin.

Leaves and rubbish were being sucked into the hole which had become bigger and wider. Crisp packets, cans, twigs disappeared into the portal and the teens struggled to keep upright, such was the pull.

A tremendous roaring sound came from it. It was like a beast coming for food. The sound increased tenfold, forcing Flo and Eddows to cover their ears from the noise.

"Look!" bellowed Eddows over the tumult. "Look into the hole!"

Flo strained her eyes into the sickening, tumbling vortex and made out, through the spiralling and clashing colours, the pale form of a woman. Her clothes billowed out around her and her hair fanned out like flames. She beckoned them to follow her into the screaming eye of the storm: it was Mary Kelly.

"I still don't believe this but it's now or never!" Grabbing Flo's hand and with his eyes tightly shut, Eddows jumped into the maw of the raging beast.

***

Eddows opened his eyes and realised that he couldn't see. He shut his eyes again, but the sensation was the same: nothing but darkness. He felt dizzy and sick; he reached out and flexed the fingers of the hand that had been attached to Flo's, wanting to feel her there as some reassurance.

Nothing.

The second pawn has arrived. The entity smiled to itself. *Let him feel my power and weep when he realises just how helpless he really is.*

Eddows opened his mouth to scream Flo's name but nothing came out. He felt rather than saw the darkness flickering around him, touching him, caressing him. He tried to pull away but found himself held fast as if he was a fly in the middle of the web of a giant spider. Eddows felt something probing his mind, nudging it, gently at first and then harder until it felt like tiny pinpricks of pain burning in his brain. Burning like ice.

"Well, well, well." The voice was soft and gentle but oh, so evil.

"Now, what have we here then? Another little one who shouldn't mess with what he doesn't understand." The voice cut through his brain, pulling and twisting at Eddows' sanity, causing the boy to flinch.

Concentrating his mind inwards he managed to croak, "Where are you?"

"I'm here."

The voice was throaty, cruel.

"All around you. Always with you. Can't you feel me here inside your head? Inside your mind. Playing with it. It's interesting in here. So many things going on. So many, many images to look at... Let me see..."

Eddows felt his brain splitting inside his skull and tried to shut out the gnawing sensation that crawled over his skin. He had to block it out. Make it stop. *Concentrate on something, anything*, thought Eddows. *Think, think, think. Think about Flo. Think about Joe. How would he deal with it? Probably better than him. Think about...*

"Trying to shut me out?" The voice rasped in his ears and Eddows found himself nodding stiffly and at the same time trying to stifle a shriek as the voice cut through his mind, shredding it again, raking at it with invisible claws.

"Oh, trying to be brave, are we? But you and I know, boy, we know that behind all that bravado, all that clever talk and perfect looks, you're scared, scared of how you really feel. Scared of what others really think."

A pause, then, "It hurts, doesn't it? Hurts to know that I know what you feel, what you think."

"I'm not scared," the boy managed to whisper back defiantly.

"I feel your fear," snickered the voice in his head and Eddows winced in pain as pinpricks of ice danced around his brain.

"What are you? Where are you from?" Even in his pain, Eddows was curious, and he reasoned, if he knew what he was up against, he could fight back, remove the pain from his mind.

Time to lie a little, the thing thought to itself. Just a small exaggeration… it wouldn't be the first time it had lied. Lies, it found, caused pain, distress and fear. It was a weapon that could hurt just as much, if not more so than physical pain. *The greeting kiss showing friendship in a garden many centuries ago had been a good lie*, the entity thought with almost wistful remembrance.

The voice wheezed and gurgled into a throaty laugh. "You really don't know me, do you?" The voice sighed in mock pity, "And you've carried me for so long. Come and embrace the darkness, child."

"What do you mean?" Eddows gasped with the effort.

"I am what I am. I am that feeling that you have every time you leave your house, looking over your shoulder. I am that sense of isolation, that feeling that'll you never fit in. Of being alone."

"I don't need you to know that! I know what I am." Eddows, despite the agony he was feeling was not going to be beaten by this thing, whatever it was. "I asked what you are, and if you are going to kill me, which you probably will, you might as well let me know. I mean, I've watched enough movies to know that the villain likes a rant about how clever and marvellous he is. Why don't you give it a go?"

The voice came again, more powerful this time. So powerful that Eddows felt his whole body vibrating with the sound. "I am anger!" spat the sound in his mind. "I am hate, despair, misery and poverty. I am all that is hopeless and forgotten. I am the smell of fear and vice and corruption. I am the taste of blood and bile. I am that which crawls, slithers and scuttles in the dark. I am fear itself. I have taught mankind what fear is. I have been so for millennia, and not just on your pathetic planet and time. You know me, boy, like all of your kind. You always have, Edward Eddows! Like I know you." The voice became a snarling roar of triumph.

Eddows' eyes flew open wide as the pressure inside his head increased until the boy felt it would explode.

"Know me as The Ripper!"

Eddows began to scream as the voice inside his head began to laugh and laugh and laugh as if it would never stop… and he felt himself drowning in the darkness.

CHAPTER EIGHT
MARY

Joe breathed heavily and sat up, pulling great gasps of air into his lungs. He threw out his arms to the floor to steady his shaking body and pulled his hands away quickly as he saw they were touching the body of the dead woman. Her eyes stared glassily up at him, unseeing. Joe resisted the urge to scream and he scurried backwards away from the corpse. He stared wildly around him. The little man who had been frozen next to him had gone. He was alone except for the body.

The moment the thing within his mind had released its grip on him he had been able to move. Joe felt cold and sick inside. Whoever, whatever had killed that woman had spoken to him. It seemed to know who he was and enjoyed playing with him. It, whatever it was, knew he was out of his time. What was strange was that as the thing had loosened its grip, he had felt another mind within his, reaching out to him. Eddows.

Did that mean that Eddows had followed him into the past and had also been caught by whatever this creature was? Joe didn't like the idea and shuddered; he had never felt so alone. He wanted his friends around him. It didn't even have to be his friends. Anyone would have done, even big bearded Lusky boy.

Suddenly he heard the sound of shouts and heavy footsteps running towards him. He looked down at his hands and saw with horror that his they were stained with the blood of the dead woman. Joe's clothes were covered with it. Whoever was coming might think he'd killed the dead lady and from what little Joe knew of this period in history, even a boy of his age would be hung for murder; he'd seen *Oliver Twist* on television. Clumsily he rubbed his hands on his top trying to wipe the sticky red substance off, but it only made matters worse.

Move! his head seemed to be saying to his frozen body. He had to move! He climbed painfully to his feet feeling stiff and cold. The woman's blood had seeped onto his trousers and had stained them a deep red colour. The smell from the corpse was overwhelming. The face of the woman continued to stare up at him with empty, dead eyes. They looked at the boy almost accusingly.

"It wasn't me…I'm sorry, but it wasn't me. Please stop looking at me, please!"

Joe was almost crying now with fear and regret.

Regret for the death of the woman mingled with the fear of what would happen to him if he was caught at the scene. Tearing himself away, Joe stumbled down the nearest dark alleyway not knowing or caring where he was going.

The footsteps behind him sounded louder now and the cries from the pursuing crowd more and more intense. He had to move faster. He remembered something that Mr. Lusk had said in one of his history lessons, "Hanging the criminal from the neck until he was dead was still the law for a murder in the 19th century. Not a particularly nice way to go, especially if the neck didn't break on the way down. When hangings were public only a few decades before, grieving relatives used to pull on the criminal's legs to help him on his way."

Joe began to sob with fear. He had never felt so frightened. Louder and louder came the cries behind him and he stumbled into the wall next to him. He let out a sharp cry as his arm scraped the wall, tearing the skin, and his shin bashed the corner of the brick as he fled down the next alley. He splashed, slid and slipped through dank, muddy puddles and through the rotting detritus that strewed the filthy cobbles. He felt he could run no more. *They will catch me*, Joe thought, *and I will hang.*

Then an arm shot out from a side alley and dragged him down it and through a narrow passage and out of sight of the closing mob.

Joe found himself in a darkened courtyard. A few straggly bushes grew up hopefully from what had once been gardens now gone with the passage of time. Dirty tenement buildings crowded in from all sides, looming over him. In the gloom, he could just make out the shape of the person who had rescued him. A slight shape, that of a woman with a torn and threadbare dress and a knotty shawl. Even though Joe couldn't make out her face, he knew who she was. "Mary Kelly!" he managed to gasp.

"Shut up!" the woman hissed at him. She pressed her ear against the brickwork and, when she was sure there was no danger, turned to Joe. "You got 'ere then. You took yer time. I wasn't sure you'd 'ave the strength, yer such a scrawny thing." A pause and a wry smile. "Looks like I was wrong."

Joe shook his head dumbly; it was all too much. He wasn't sure he understood. In fact, he was sure that he didn't understand anything at the moment.

"Come on!"

The woman grabbed his arm again and pulled him into the nearest building. She dragged him up a set of steep and rotting

71

stairs, down a narrow corridor and through a door into a small but smelly darkened room and then pushed him down onto an ancient bed that creaked alarmingly even under his light weight.

Joe sat, dazed and confused, as the woman bustled about him and rootled through a small cupboard, produced a stub of candle and lit it. A warm glow filled the room and Joe could see that it wasn't much better in the light. If anything, it was worse.

He took a good look at the woman. She was quite young, but her face was hard, as if she had seen things she wasn't meant to have seen. Wild red hair framed her face and hung down in dirty curtains around a pale face. The woman looked at the boy with the largest pair of brown eyes that Joe had ever seen. A snub nose and a full mouth, set firm, completed the picture.

"Where are we?"

"Safe, for the moment. Even a mob like the one chasing you won't dare come up 'ere." Mary's voice was full of contempt.

"No," said Joe in a small voice, "I mean, where are we, exactly?"

"26 Dorset Street, East London. Our little rookeries is what the law calls 'em. And this, my lad, is my home." The woman ran her hand gently over the battered bedstead and gazed at the room a little sadly.

"Then you… You are…" he managed to mouth. "You are Mary Kelly."

"Don't think I should know it?" Mary moved closer to him. "I was born with the name, so I should know. And you are Mr. Joe, I 'ope, or it weren't worth the risk of getting you 'ere." The voice was surprisingly rich and held just a trace of mocking laughter.

"Yes, I'm Joe."

The boy held his head in his hands and breathed deeply. Mary waited for the boy to calm down.

"This is mad. This just can't be happening. All of this is just some kind of sick dream… no, nightmare."

Joe shook his head as if to clear it. "I know who you are. The whole of East London knows who you are. Hell, I should think most of the world knows. And you should be dead." The words were out of his mouth before he could stop them.

"Jesus, Mary and Joseph! Is that how you chat up all the girls, is it? Shame really. You is quite a sweet-looking little gentleman if you kept yer mouth shut." Kelly jutted her jaw out attractively.

Joe felt himself going red, it seemed to be becoming a habit. "I'm sorry. I didn't mean for it to…"

"What? To tell the truth? You know it as well as I do; by the end of all this I'll be dead." Mary sounded so matter of fact.

"I didn't think…how do you know…" Joe was more confused than he had been in his life. His head was hurting more than ever. More than it did in an English comprehension test and those were just the worst.

"What? That I know I'm gonna die? I know I am. I know I've got to. Can't change the past. Can't change what is gonna 'appen. But it's not gonna 'appen yet. Not just yet. I've still a little time."

Kelly's face changed, became sad, her voice wistful, almost dreamy. "That girl who was lying dead back there in Berner Street, she knew too. Poor Lizzie, she thought she 'ad more time. Just like the others."

Joe didn't know what to say. He had been suddenly taken at how this woman was so matter of fact that she had known she was the living-dead.

"How do you know my name, then? Why have all these weird things been happening to me? Why the hell am I here?"

He could feel himself becoming angry. He was sorry that Mary Kelly would die and that other lady, Lizzie she'd been called, was dead too, he really was, but what had that to do with him? He was fed up of not knowing what was going on, of being kept in the dark. And what the hell had messed with his head back there in the street? As if she was anticipating the question, Mary spoke.

"Didn't you feel it, back there in the alley, as it took yer mind?"

"Feel what?"

"The hatred. The sadness and despair. That voice you 'eard in your head is…" The tone was sad, gentle even. But how could that be, when she must have known the pain that it had caused Joe.

"The Ripper?"

Mary nodded in reply to Joe's question.

"I know all about him. Some madman that killed you… and other people, I mean, and no one ever caught him."

Joe's puzzlement grew. The way that Mary spoke of things wasn't the way he had expected her to.

"Nah. That's where you is wrong, young man."

Mary moved towards the candle, as if the light and warmth was giving her strength.

"It ain't no person, that Ripper. It's *feelings*, that's what it is and that's what I think anyhow. Feelings given strength and form

74

through the fears of others. It feeds off them. I don't know how or what it really is, or even what part I play in all this, but what I do know is that I'm the link between my time and yours. I'm a warning if you like, that if you ain't careful it's gonna happen again in your time. And you, Joe, are the other link, and you need to be the one who stops it."

Joe could feel his head beginning to spin. He didn't understand. He had learnt at school that the Ripper was a serial killer who seemed to kill for the fun of it. This now was something different altogether.

"I don't follow. I don't get it. Why me?" Joe bunched his sticky, bloodied hands against his temples trying desperately to fight back tears. He knew he sounded pathetic, but he had no idea what was going on. Then again, at school he never had any idea what was going on, so maybe it wasn't all that different.

Except there no one wanted him dead.

"Like I say there's no Ripper, at least not what you think it to be. You 'ad a good look around you while you were 'ere?" Joe nodded and remembered all the squalor and dirt and grinding poverty he had witnessed since he had arrived in this time.

"Then you saw what this place, what we who live in it 'ave become. The feelings of all them people had grown, givin' it food, strength until it could reach out and gain a foothold in our world. The street, Dorset Street, it's alive. Something was bound there, long, long ago in the very fabric of the buildings, the earth and very stone itself. Kept tied up tight forever. Or that's 'ow it should've been. But look, Joe, look around yer at the rubbish we live in." Mary paused and stared out of the dirt-covered window at the filthy walls outside. She turned back to him.

"Whatever it was, it felt the fear and despair of all them poor souls that lived 'ere and has been able to get out, at least in a limited way. It grew strong on them fears. It felt. It lived. It killed. It felt good. And it won't be stopped. And it is coming again. It came for Martha, Pol and Annie. Then it came for poor Lizzie. And now it's coming for me. All that hatred, all that evil, from the past… And it won't be stopped until it has consumed you all."

CHAPTER NINE
WHAT IS FEAR?

It felt, rather than saw the final piece in the Game. Felt her fear as she came closer. It would show her its power now that the new vessel was ready. A smaller, weaker vessel certainly, but perfectly serviceable none the less. It would do for the moment until the world would be ready to feel its power once again...

"Eddows! Eddows! Where are you?" Her voice sounded so small and insignificant as Flo stumbled through the darkness, blindly groping her way along. Her head and her heart were pounding, and she felt as if her stomach had been rearranged. Without warning the floor dropped away from her and she found herself half falling, half sliding down a narrow passage until she landed on the dirt and debris of a dank room.

Flo sat up groggily and looked around her. It was dark, but there was a faint light coming from somewhere. She saw that she was in a crumbling brick room that seemed to be divided into two by a gothic style archway. The light was coming from the other side of the arch.

The side she was sitting in was bare, save rotting straw and rubbish: half-collapsed boxes, food waste and brown stuff she didn't really want to think about too much, although she didn't need to think about it. She could smell it, and what she smelt, smelt bad. The light itself was a sickly blue colour that flickered and pulsed as if it were alive. It made Flo feel afraid.

A cold, empty afraid, although she didn't know why.

Flo crept softly across the room, wincing as something black and hairy ran squeaking across her foot, until she was at the edge of the archway. She peered round. What she saw made her hands fly to her mouth, forget the mess, forget the smell, forget the dark. Flo had always loved horror films but they were only pretend. She'd never had nightmares about one. All fake blood, plastic limbs and a body count of beautiful people who couldn't act from US daytime soap operas. Now she felt, looking at what she could see, that the nightmare was real and would never stop.

It was another stone room much like the one she had just entered from. Dirty, dank and dark save for the sickly blue glow. A wooden doorway to the far end and another offshoot that looked like some kind of study to the right, but Flo couldn't quite make out the details. In any case, it wasn't the room that made Flo forget the dark.

It was the boy on the ceiling.

Edward Eddows was suspended face down in the air, arms and legs pulled out as if he had been staked out to die in some god-forsaken desert, head thrown back at a grotesque angle, almost like his neck had been broken. Flames of nauseating blue and green light, which to Flo resembled strands of an immense spider's web, held him there, twisting and writhing with obscene sticky life. Eddows' handsome face was pale and contorted, his normally blue eyes empty and bulging white like boiled eggs. It appeared as if he had been drained of all life. But it was his mouth that was the most dreadful sight.

Hanging open, an enormous black hole in the empty white, a silent scream, as if he was drooling, and from it, writhing and wriggling, like the tentacles of a squid, were ribbons of darkness.

78

Drawing her eyes away from the sickening image, Flo looked round the rest of the room. The sight that greeted her was no better. On the dirty floor around her were decaying human skeletons and others that looked like animals. Some were complete, some just fragments of rotted bone and they were all old, so old...She wondered how they had come to be here in this dreadful place and what had happened to them. Flo looked back at Eddows. He hadn't moved and she wondered if he could hear her.

"Eddows." Her voice sounded small and pathetic. "Eddows! It's me, Flo! Can you hear me?"

"Oh, he can hear you, child."

The voice had the sound of rust and dirt and age.

Flo felt her body go rigid with fear and the hairs on the back of her neck stand on end. The voice had not come from Eddows; it seemed to come from all corners of that filthy room, from the very bricks themselves. Her eyes glanced wildly around but she could see nothing. The atmosphere in the room was oppressive, heavy and Flo felt as if it was beginning to crush her.

"He can hear you and it's breaking his heart to know that he can't help you. Because he knows what's coming next and he won't be able to stop himself!"

The voice came from all sides at once. It sounded like one or many voices all trying to break free.

"What?" Flo tried hard to keep the fear and shaking horror from her voice. "What's coming next?"

"Fear is coming. The fear that he feels when he kills you, my little one."

The voice was matter of fact and almost regretful. Flo was sure that mixed amongst its rough tones was that of a woman.

"You are going be the next to feel the hands of fear, of hate, of pain as they crush you and tear your soul from you."

"Eddows is my friend. He wouldn't hurt me!" Flo cried sounding braver than she felt.

"I know, but he won't be able to stop himself. He'll hate himself when he squeezes the life out of you and then leaves your body to the rats."

Flo screamed and hot tears ran down her cheeks. She clenched her fists and felt her nails in her fists pierce her skin. Her heart felt as if it would burst as she watched Eddows descend through the air to the floor blocking the doorway beyond, lowered by the twisting, pulsating web that held him. The boy's eyes were empty, empty like those of the dead. Dead like she was going to be.

Flo backed away until she could feel the cold, wet stone of the wall behind her. There was nowhere else to go. The voice from the walls laughed wildly.

"WHO ARE YOU? Why are you doing this? Please, I don't..." her scream became a sob that died in her throat as the body of Eddows began to lurch towards her, mouth open spewing blackness like oil.

"Can you feel the fear now?" the voice within her mind and without seemed to cry. "Can you feel the hopeless misery and poverty of generations that live within me?"

"Please, please, Eddows, not me..." Flo cowered away from the hideous sight.

Eddows' body halted in front of her, like some hideous marionette. The atmosphere in the room lessened slightly, the blue light flickered and pulsed, faded almost, as if whatever it was, had become distracted by something.

"You're right. Not now. Not here. One more tonight. One more rip. But not you. Not yet. The Game must be played." The disembodied voice murmured softly.

Then, "Oh, very well. Have him!"

Eddows' body flew through the air like a rag doll thrown casually aside by a child and crashed into the wall, slid down it, and lay in a crumpled and broken heap on the floor. Flo watched in mounting horror as it convulsed and wretched, as if Eddows was trying to vomit whilst having a fit. The body jerked upright, and the boy's mouth opened unnaturally wide as tendrils of darkness spewed forth from it. Flo covered her face from the repulsive miasma as it spiralled around her and upward and into the fabric of the walls before disappearing, running into the very stone.

Flo looked back to the body of Eddows, which had slumped back onto the floor. She crawled over to him and sat watching the fallen boy for what seemed like an eternity. At first, she had a terrible thought he was dead, until she detected the faint rise and fall from his stomach. He was still pale, but some colour was beginning to come back to his cheeks.

Flo took a deep breath and shuffled over to Eddows and tentatively shook his shoulder. There was no response from the boy, so she tried again harder this time.

"Eddows," she whispered. "Please, please, please. Are you all right?"

Flo was rewarded this time as from the prone boy on the floor came a low groan followed by a coughing fit. She watched as Eddows rolled onto his side and vomited out a thick, black mud-like fluid and, to her disgust, flies and other insect forms. Suddenly angry at what had happened to her friend, she leapt upwards and crushed the vermin under her foot, grinding them to slime and dust, screaming as she did so.

Eddows rolled around on the floor crying and clutching his stomach, spitting out the last of the rubbish from him.

"Flo, Flo, Flo!" The boy was now sobbing uncontrollably, tears running like rivers down his dirty cheeks. Flo knelt down by him and cradled the boy in her arms. It felt good, she thought suddenly, to hold him.

Slowly the sobbing subsided and Eddows was still, save for the wracking breathing that seemed to almost tear his whole body apart. At last, he sat up and Flo was relieved to see that his eyes were back to their usual deep blue colour.

"Oh, Flo, I'm so sorry. I could see you and how frightened you were, and I just couldn't stop myself. It controlled my movements, my mind. I couldn't stop… Oh, God, it was horrible."

Flo cuddled him tight.

"It's okay. I know it wasn't you, you were taken over by that…that thing." She stopped and looked puzzled. "But why did it stop?"

Eddows rubbed his eyes as if seeing her for the first time and shook his head. "I don't know. I could feel it squeezing my mind and then it was as if it became distracted suddenly. Like it had something else to do. Then it, well, let go."

Flo looked thoughtful and then her eyes opened wide with fear. "It said it had something to do. One more to do tonight… Oh! Eddows, it didn't mean?"

Somewhere, out there, in the dark heart of Victorian London, something terrible was happening.

CHAPTER TEN
ANOTHER MURDER

Joe sat looking out of the window watching the lights of London glowing through the murky pane. Even in the dirt and despair that seemed to be etched upon the very fabric of the place in which he sat, Joe couldn't help but be bedazzled by the city in which he lived, in whatever period. In the distance, he could see the squat stone form of London Bridge lit with smoky gas lamps, and beyond that the smear that was the Houses of Parliament.

The rain had subsided and, despite the smell of decay that hung in every corner of the room, the night was, for once, clear. London looked from here the most wonderful city in the world. But Joe knew different. Joe knew what lay beneath the façade of the jewel in the crown of the 'glorious' British Empire, an Empire that at this moment covered half the globe at the expense of the poor and couldn't be bothered to sort out its own problems closer to home. *Same old, same old*, he thought.

"Beautiful, ain't it?"

The voice of Mary Kelly interrupted his thoughts and he turned his head to see her standing beside the bed looking out at the sight.

"Even in this godforsaken mess me and others are in, there are times when I look out there and think that there is some hope, some small glimmer or spark that'll end all this fear and misery. It's not all bad. There are people who want to help people like me, but we are too proud to take it half the time. We prefer to be what we are."

"That's what that thing said." Joe shuddered as he remembered the feeling of black hopelessness in the yard. "I am what I am."

"I am what I am," repeated Mary softly. "I like that. Yeah, I like that. Like it means something."

Joe watched as Mary gathered herself together, pulled her shawl around her shoulders and shivered slightly. "A clear night is all well and good, Joe, but at least the smog and fog keeps the heat in. Freezing, isn't it? I've got to go out for a bit, you wait here until I come back."

Joe turned to her and felt his face go hot. "Working then?"

He felt a mixture of satisfaction and guilt as he saw Mary go almost as red as he felt.

"If you like. I gotta live, ain't I? It pays its way…" Then an angry torrent spewed forth. "You don't know what it's like, do yer? You 'ave no idea what it's like to be me. To be us. Only we girls know what it's like. And look at some of them! Dead! Dead like I'm gonna be!"

Joe was too startled to reply and before he could utter any kind of apology, Mary was gone, slamming the door behind her. He turned to the window and strained to look down to see if he could see Mary. To his horror, the fog had now returned, creeping in and filling the empty passageways and alleys below. He could feel the air beginning to thicken, almost pressing against the pane, as if Mary's anger had caused it to return. He jumped off the bed and out of the door in pursuit of Mary.

The fog hemmed Joe in on all sides as he stumbled along the narrow passages that linked Dorset Street to the main thoroughfare. He could barely see two feet ahead, his outstretched arms in front of him as he groped his way blindly forward. How could anyone see to do anything in this fog?

Joe cursed loudly as he scraped his hands over rough stone, feeling hot tears spring from his eyes as the blood ran down his wrist. He stumbled and fell to the floor under a spluttering gas lamp. Joe looked down at his hand and saw that the cut was deep, the skin pulled back almost like a smile. Pulling his hankie from his pocket, he bound the wound as tightly as he could, wincing as he did so.

And then he felt it.

Pressure hit him like an immense weight that pushed him to the ground. He struggled to move as he felt something pass over him. The Angel of Death? Hadn't he heard the story from the Bible when he was little? That the Angel of Death had killed all the first-born Egyptian boys? He wasn't an Egyptian and this wasn't the Bible, but this was surely Death.

The darkness and coldness were intense, and Joe could hardly breathe. He felt the pressure increase around his neck and then he was thrown over, so he was facing upwards towards the black sky.

Some form was sitting on him! A form made of smoke, dirt and filth. A shadowy form, much like before, but this time it was more distinct. It was human-shaped, wearing what appeared to be late Victorian evening wear, complete with a tall top hat. There were still no features; it was still like a thick mist.

"Well, told you I'd be seeing you again, boy." Joe couldn't even scream, so heavy was the feeling on him. The voice was the same as before but stronger somehow.

"What do you think of my shape, eh? Good? I've been hearing all the news about me with interest. I seem to have caused quite a stir around here, much like I did centuries before. It's a shame you cannot see my true form, but then it would drive you mad! They are calling me the 'Ripper,' the descendent of Spring-Heeled Jack, the mad son of Royalty. The pictures of me are wonderfully descriptive, which is why I rather like this shape. Noble, don't you think? Or not?"

The shape paused, as if waiting for the stricken boy to answer.

"Or can't you talk?"

Joe struggled hard, but it was no use. He was going to die here, out of his time and no one would know about it. Joe could feel the saliva in his mouth choking him and his eyes rolled helplessly in his head as the sound of thunder pounded in his ears.

"You can stop struggling," the voice hissed in his ear. "I'm not going to kill you…yet. I've even let your friends live. I've got other things to play out in this Game and I need you alive. For now."

Joe was flung through the air and landed with a thump against the wall. He felt his body crack as he slid down it and into merciful oblivion.

"Joe! Wake up! You can't sleep out here!"

Joe heard the familiar voice shouting down his left ear. His head hurt. He wanted to go back to sleep, back to the darkness and quiet. To his annoyance the voice continued to shout and then a pair of hands started to shake him.

"Bog off!" he murmured and waved his arms pathetically like a seal.

"Nothing wrong with him, then. His choice of language relating to all things scatological and juvenile is present and correct." another voice that was also very familiar smirked.

Joe wearily opened his eyes and saw what he had suspected: Flo and Eddows staring down at him, Flo's face concerned and set, Eddows with the merest flicker of a smile on his lips.

"You all right?" Flo said as Joe struggled to his feet. He brushed off their aid and shook himself down. He felt cold and numb but that was all. There were no bones broken but his bloodied hand hurt and throbbed like hell.

"I'm fine. How did you get here?" he managed to croak, rubbing his sore body with his one good hand.

"We followed you through to wherever the hell we are…and judging by the look of this place, we might as well be." Eddows replied, taking in the view of the crumbling tenements and rotting housing that surrounded them.

"Dorset Street."

The words rang hollowly through the air. The fog had gone, to be replaced with a clear, icy chill.

"Yes, that place you've been going on and on about and so here we are. So maybe you can now explain what is going on?"

Joe shook his head and sighed deeply. He wanted to explain what he knew, to be clear, but he knew it would all sound rubbish to the other two. He took a deep breath…

***

"So, let me get this right. This, this thing that knows we're here, out of our time and possibly could be Jack the Ripper, is letting us live for the moment for some reason known only to whatever it is. And this Mary Kelly, wherever she is now, wants us here to stop what is happening now from happening again, but we can't, because whatever this thing is, we can't fight it. We don't know how to get back to our own time to stop it killing again and until then we're stuck here."

Flo paused for breath and looked at the two boys staring blankly at her. She'd summed up everything beautifully, she'd thought, and all she was getting was black holes like the Blackwell Tunnel.

"Yeah. That just about sums it up," Joe said flatly.

"We need answers, then."

Eddows had had enough of standing around doing nothing. He wanted answers and all the time something was telling him that they needed to see Mary Kelly again. And besides, it was cold standing there in the middle of the street.

"The only person we can talk to here, other than the killer, of course, is Mary Kelly. And from what you said, Joe, we'd better be quick, because from the sound of it, her days are numbered."

"Then let's go." Joe had also begun to worry about Mary. At that moment, a police whistle rent the air, followed by the sound of running feet and the shout of voices.

"We may be too late," Eddows said, glancing upwards towards the noise. "Come on!"

The threesome ran down the alley and into the darkness beyond. The night had claimed another victim.

***

More shouts and cries rent the air as Joe, Flo, and Eddows entered another dark street indistinguishable from the last. Sounds, murmurs came at them like ghosts on the wind.

"Another one! Another murder. How terrible!"

"What are we gonna do? The police ain't got no clue who's responsible."

"Bloody useless, that's what they is!"

And above it all the sound of mocking laughter echoing from alley to alley.

As the three reached the scene, a large crowd had gathered around the body of the woman that lay in Mitre Square. Joe noticed the same faces as before: men still in their working gear with grim, set faces. Women in dirty dresses and shawls gossiping in small groups, children craning to see what fresh horror the night had given them to scare younger siblings.

The young man with the lank, greasy hair, retching into the gutter. He looked worse than before if that was possible, paler and with blank, glassy eyes. The man must have realised that Joe was staring at him because he gave the boy such a look that Joe lowered his eyes. The face was full of pain, regret and something else? Something not quite human flickering behind the eyes. Joe couldn't work out what it was.

Maybe the man was a friend of the murdered woman? When he looked again, the young man seemed to be shaking his head, as if in pain, before slipping away, merging with the shadows. From their position at the back of the crowd the teens had a suspicion that this murder was a particularly brutal one. Blood was staining the cobbles in great patches and many of the women were crying and in distress.

Joe noticed Mary hovering at the back of the crowd and made his way through the throng towards her. He touched her lightly on the arm but there was no reaction. He tried again.

"I'm sorry," he said simply.

"Poor Catherine," murmured Mary, appearing not to have heard Joe. "Poor, poor Catherine. She knew it was coming, like we all knew, but who'd have thought it would happen on the same night as Liz. Our numbers grow thin."

She turned and looked at Joe.

"Oh, hello, Joe," Mary said. "It's me next."

CHAPTER ELEVEN
I MET A MAN

The threesome half led, half dragged Mary back to her dwelling in Dorset Street, taking care to avoid the milling crowds. Joe had the feeling that he was being watched and glanced quickly around him. He saw the shape of a man step back around the corner of the street and Joe swore he saw green eyes glowing in the darkness. *Another mystery*, Joe thought, *that will have to wait for now.*

The shock of seeing another of her friends butchered in such a terrible way had affected Mary deeply and she had begun to ramble in a strange tongue like another language. When they could understand what she was saying it was mostly rubbish concerning her childhood and her friends from long ago.

At last they reached her room and laid the woman down on the bed. Mary fell asleep, and although she tossed and turned, she did not wake. Flo, Joe, and Eddows sat on the side of the bed and watched her. They did not speak. They didn't know what to say. Even Eddows was at a loss for words. They were all shaken by the events of that night, and although exhausted, were too terrified to sleep.

Joe was confused. Just who was the man with green eyes? And for some reason, he couldn't get the image of the young man with lank hair out of his mind. He had looked much the same as before but there had been something wrong with the side of his head as he had shaken it; it had looked deformed, almost...

The first fingers of dawn light crept over London, spilling through the window. The paling sky lifted Joe's heart slightly as if he knew that the killer would not strike during daylight, preferring the cloaked shroud of night to perform its grisly deeds.

He looked at the faces of the other two, dirty, pale and drawn, and knew that he and they were getting near the end of their strength. Too much had happened to them over the last few days and it surprised him that they were all still holding it together.

He sat and thought hard. There was something about all this that puzzled him. When he had been communicating with the "thing," he had felt something touch him deeply. It was as if whatever it was had been around for centuries, the weight of ages and time lost forever, an ancient being travelling through time, killing, moving on, alone. Alone. So alone. It was so very alone.

Joe wondered where it had come from and he almost felt a pity for the thing, whatever it turned out to be. To be so angry, angry enough to kill and enjoy the feeling. Then he remembered what it had done to Mary's friends and what it would go on to do. The feeling of pity was replaced with a feeling of intense hatred that made his stomach lurch. He was surprised that he could feel that way about anything.

***

Flo was asleep when Eddows shouted, "I've got it! I know what that thing it is! I know how it works! God, I'm a genius! I'd have waited an eternity for you two muppets to even come close!"

The girl saw Joe turn and look with a stunned expression at Eddows, whose face was alight with triumph and he was hopping from foot to foot with excitement.

"It's been written about throughout the centuries. It has been here forever. Well, if not forever, at least for a very long time. Don't you see?"

Two blank faces stared at him. Eddows tutted impatiently to himself. Such a pair of morons.

"Ah. I thought not." He began to explain.

"It's always been here, in this place! This 'thing' that is systematically killing Mary's friends and, no doubt other poor people throughout time, is London."

Eddows paused and was really rather miffed that they hadn't understood. It was all so very simple. Sometimes these two were really beneath him. Eddows sighed and tried again. He had been right the first time. Morons.

"Written about by Edgar Allen Poe. Come on, Flo, you like horror stories, you might at least have heard of him. Joe, you wouldn't get it—you don't read." Eddows realised what he had said and reddened with embarrassment.

"Sorry, that was unfair... It was a short story in 1840. Called 'The Man of the Crowd.' The narrator of the story follows an old man that goes through all the types of places and people in London. At the end of the story, he realises that he has been following the 'embodiment' of the crowd. That the man is actually the spirit of London. Oh, what's the line... 'of vast mental power... of coolness, of malice'."

Both Joe and Flo still looked blank and Eddows groaned at having to deal with two such cretins but felt something within him was asking him to try again.

"We are fighting a spirit. A spirit made up of all the horror and misery in this period of London. No? That poem we did in English last term. The one by Hughes Mearns…remember? Yesterday, upon the stair, 'I met a man upon the stair, I met a man who wasn't there, he wasn't there again today, I wish, I wish he'd go away.' Think!" Eddows struck the table with his fist making the other two jump.

"Think, you two! It, this spirit thing, feeds on people's emotions when things are at their worst. When the population is at rock bottom. When misery and hatred are so strong that the spirit gains power: power that destroys and kills."

Joe and Flo looked at each other and then back at the smug, smiling Edward Eddows.

"Hell, Eddows. You are brilliant!" Joe shouted at him. "How the hell did you work it out? Hell, I thought you were just a boff job with a stupid name."

"So many 'hells' in one sentence, Joe. Be careful you don't use up your daily quota of words," Eddows shot back.

"Joe, shut up!" Flo elbowed the boy in the ribs. "That's great O Jedi, the only thing you haven't got to yet is what it all has to do with us? Why are we here?"

"Oh." Eddows' smile slipped from his face and he felt himself deflate. "I hadn't thought of that".

Despite this, Joe couldn't help grinning at the fact Eddows wasn't as smart as he thought he was. Moron.

"It's 'im," came a quavering voice from the bed. The three turned to see Mary struggling to sit up. One limp hand was pointing at Joe. "It's 'im. Joe is yer link to all this. Us girls, we brought 'im back to stop this from happening again. That thing out there won't be satisfied with me. It's growing stronger. And only Joe can stop it!"

CHAPTER TWELVE
REVELATIONS

"What do you mean, I'm a link?" gasped Joe. "I've never met you before. I'm not a link. You are all bloody mad! I want out of this!"

Eddows laid a calming hand on the trembling Joe's shoulder. "Remember, you're not on your own in all this, you've got Flo and I."

"Marvellous. A goth and a boff. Doomed," came the reply.

Flo was speaking quietly to Mary. "We can't save you, can we? We can't undo the past."

Mary smiled weakly at Flo and lay back down on the bed. Her latest outburst had seemed to drain the strength from her. She looked so small lying there on the rumpled quilt. "No, love. What 'as happened 'ere can't not happen. I'm gonna die just like Liz and Cath, and there's nothing you or anyone else can do about it. We brought you 'ere to stop it in the future; me and my girls, we knew what was coming. Anyway, it was our fault."

Eddows squinted at Mary. "Your fault? All this stuff that will come out later, about the murders being Kabbalistic magic."

Joe gave the boy a quizzical look. Eddows rolled his eyes.

"It's from the Jewish religion. Jewish magic, if you like. You and your girls are Jewish descendants, isn't that right? Or at least interested in that part of the Jewish way of life. That's what you were speaking earlier. Yiddish, the language of the Jews."

Mary nodded. "We were all part of a coven. Thought it would be a bit of fun…thought we might make a difference. A few spells 'ere and there to give some 'ope to those without any. In the end, we let out whatever is calling itself the Ripper."

"So, there was no plot or cover up by the Royals, or anything like that about Jack the Ripper," Eddows said. "You released whatever that thing is and now you're paying the price in trying to stop it."

"Sharp, I'll give yer friend that. And we'll fail. But you lot. You are the last hope." Mary struggled off the bed and towards the window. She looked out at the view, smiled sadly and sighed deeply.

"I've less than two months left before I die. I ain't frightened. I don't fear death or what happens after. I know there are places better than this. Worlds that aren't full of darkness."

The words made Joe think again about the man on the street corner, the man in the pub. The man with the strange green eyes. He'd said something similar. Who was he and how did he fit into this, if he did at all? He dragged his thoughts back to the present.

"Eddows said you were witches?" Flo was saying. "Can't you magic yourself out of all this?"

Mary laughed and slapped her hands down on her knees, "What and use me cat to scratch out its eyes? Lord love yer, girl. We don't go flying around on broomsticks and stuff. No, we deal in feelings and stuff. Herbs and flowers, signs and symbols. The odd love potion too, but no real hocus-pocus. I say we, but there ain't too many of us left."

"Then…the killer? You know what it is?" Eddows leaned forward, eager for more knowledge.

"That was an accident. Some man heard we was into magic and stuff like. Gave us this book, looked magic, he said. Had a yellow star on the front, like that magician might 'ave down the Music Hall. Didn't want nuffing for it, neither."

"Who was he?" asked Joe, feeling that he knew the answer.

"Don't know. Never saw him before, or since."

"Did he have green eyes?"

Mary looked sharply at Joe. "'Ow'd you know that?" she asked.

"Just a guess." Joe felt his stomach turn and the hair lifting on the back of his neck.

"Never mind that. Go on," probed Eddows. "What happened next?"

"We couldn't read it, not being educated like youse is. In the end one of the girls contacted a bloke called John Druitt…"

Joe sat bolt upright and grabbed Flo's hand so hard she cried out in pain.

"Druitt! Christ! That's my name! That's my family name. Why didn't you say?"

Mary smiled wanly. "I haven't really had the chance, have I? It's been a little busy."

Eddows pushed the excited and confused Joe back down on the bed. He turned back to Mary and waved a finger in the general direction of the bouncing Joe to be quiet and listen.

"And? I assume you met him? What did he say?" Eddows was insistent.

Joe looked narrowly him. He knew Eddows had a thirst for knowledge, but this was too forceful, too in your face. Maybe being possessed by that creature had touched him somehow.

"It wasn't so much what he said as what he did," Mary was saying. "He told us he could unlock the writings and the book was far older than what we 'ad thought. He said he was a warlock or wizard and could help us. We'd heard of such people up Essex way. George Pickergill of Canewdon and such like. Druitt told us that he'd done all this before. We didn't have any reason to disbelieve him. The Jewish community has always had Kabbalist wizards here."

Flo interrupted the flow with a wave of her hand.

"Hang on. So, you girls were curious over some old writings that someone you didn't know gave you? That your curiosity caused all this mess? All this madness?" She stood up, suddenly sickened with it all. "What happened next?" she asked simply.

"'E said that book was from the time of the Great Plague of London. It 'ad all sorts of weird stuff written in it. Talked about strange things and creatures from another world. Druitt said that a great evil came here in the form of a spirit."

"You mean a demon?" cut in Eddows.

"If you like. London had become the most decadent city in the world, that the spirit or demon, was growing in power and that the city needed cleansing and stuff. The magic in the book could be used to bind the creature tight again like it had been before. Us girls thought we could do something positive for once. You've seen what it's like for us, living 'ere."

The threesome shuffled uncomfortably. Living in the East End at this time must have been tough and they could understand the women wanting a way out, a better future. Flo felt bad at her outburst before as Mary continued.

"Druitt needed some of our...blood as a Contract with the creature. Well, six of us gave it him. He then added his own blood to the book to complete the ritual. The blood was supposed to bind the thing. He said that he would be able to talk to it, communicate with it. Find out where it was from. Curiosity killed the cat." Mary smiled sadly again. "And soon it'll kill me too."

Flo looked at Mary as if seeing her differently. "So, you mean, that if you hadn't been so curious none of this would have happened? We wouldn't have been dragged here and scared out of our wits. Joe wouldn't have seen things no one is meant to see and Eddows here wouldn't have been possessed by a demon?" Somewhere in an adjoining tenement a baby had started wailing, followed by a male voice shouting at it to be quiet.

"No, love." Mary's voice was gentle. "It would have been released sooner or later." She took a deep breath and carried on. "We all met at midnight in this very street and Druitt read out this incantation. Made no sense to us. Then nothing. We thought he was having us on. Then this hole, I can't describe it really, seemed to open in the wall. There were things... things in there. Almost like another world...the colours were so bright, so beautiful."

"Like a wormhole to another time and place." Eddows' eyes were bright. "Druitt opened a portal to another dimension. These things *are* possible. It's...it's incredible." He turned to Mary and shook her shoulder gently. "What happened next?"

"Suddenly, we all felt this enormous pressure on us, weighing us down. The pitch darkness of midnight round 'ere was nothing compared to what happened next." Mary's voice took on a singsong quality and tears began to stream down her face. Joe, moving to comfort her, took hold of her hand.

"Well, what did happen?" Eddows was anxious to get to the end.

"We were all flung against the wall by some force. It began to speak through Druitt's wife. He'd brought her along, too; men always want to show off."

Flo shivered as she remembered how the thing had used Eddows and spoken through him with that strange grating voice.

"Druitt couldn't stop it," murmured Mary. "He tried to undo what he had started but couldn't. You should have seen it. It was the most 'orrific thing I've ever seen. I'll never be able to describe it. Anyhow, Druitt did what he could as we all stood there crying and screaming. The best he could do was to bind it into the very stones of Dorset Street. The whole street seemed to change as 'e did it. Becoming this, this *monster*. It started then speaking to us through the very stones. Druitt 'ad put it in. It said that it had waited many years to reach its full power. It had been able to influence people's feelings, discontentment, hatred and suchlike, the occasional killing, but that was all. But now the incantation that 'ad been cast allowed it limited freedom but soon it would be completely free. It would use us as an example and destroy us to show the world what it was capable of doing—but it could only kill us as we were contracted to it. It would feed on us first. Consume us in the most barbaric way possible, using others to do it."

Mary turned eyes like lead to the window and looked out. "Look at how many of us are dead already"

Joe squeezed Mary's hand gently. "What happened next?"

The woman shook her head, "We all fled, like the cowards and rats we were, leaving Druitt alone."

She began to weep quietly.

"What happened to him? Did he die?" Joe asked, his voice flat as he thought of the terrible fear that Druitt, one of his ancestors, must have felt facing the demon. "What happened to Druitt?"

Mary wiped her eyes on her shawl, pulled herself together and shrugged her shoulders. "We asked around the next day. No one knew where 'e was. We 'eard some bits and pieces of information; he had gone to ground, left his wife. So 'e's not dead but might as well be."

"Druitt? Hang on! Is he young with black hair? Sort of greasy looking?" Joe asked Mary. She nodded miserably and stared up at him.

"What? 'ave you seen 'im?" Mary asked, clutching Joe's arm.

"I've seen him", Joe said grimly. "Waiting there, watching there in the dark. At each murder, he was there watching, retching...I wonder..."

"What about his wife?" Flo asked Mary, bringing the conversation back on track.

Mary looked at the floor, swishing the dust and dirt with a shoe. "She got sent to Bedlam. She got committed to the nut 'ouse. They found 'er not long after we'd left. Sat rocking, she was, and crying silent tears. She'd gone mad after what she saw."

Joe nodded grimly. "So where do we...I...fit into all this? I know now Druitt's my ancestor and all...but how did you get us here?"

"The thing left with it a kind of stain... a sort of rip in time, looked like some dirty mark on a picture. Wherever that thing went, it used it as a kind of tunnel. Like a rat down a trap. We followed it through and saw our own deaths. It was as if it was taunting us about what was to come. It then made its first and only mistake... it left the rip open once it had been through. We

101

could see what it had been in the past, like the Great Plague, and also what it could be in the future. We didn't have dates or anything, just a sense of place. Like loads of doorways to everywhere. That's how we found you. We couldn't step through to your time as we would never exist there, but an object that had been touched by us would allow us there as a sort of image."

"That explains the violets then," breathed Eddows. "You used them as a touchstone to gain a foothold in our reality. But that doesn't explain what we are supposed to do now. What's happened in the past stays in the past. We can't change anything. It's history."

Mary slumped forward on the bed as if the effort of her story had been too much. She held her head in her hands and began to sob again. "We didn't know what would happen! How could we? Most of us are just working girls! It was something different; something exciting."

"Don't mess with things you don't understand," Joe whispered through gritted teeth. "You've cursed my family for generations."

"It's not like that!" Mary looked up, her eyes bright with tears. "It don't work that way! It would have found some other way through, despite us. And if it hadn't been you, it would have been someone else."

"You tried to warn the community, didn't you?" Eddows' voice was low and hard. "I remember reading that on the wall next to the body of Liz was written the words, 'The Juwes are The Men that Will not be Blamed for nothing.' You had enough education to have written that. Except no one understood what you meant. Who wrote it? You or…"

"Cath wrote it before she died." Mary began to sob uncontrollably again and Flo, all anger for the woman and what she and her friends had done dissolved to pity, took her hand and stroked it gently.

"We need to find Druitt," muttered Eddows to Joe, who nodded briefly in agreement.

Joe walked over towards the sobbing Mary and sat down gently on the bed next to her. He picked up her other hand in his, noticing just how dirty and bruised her hands were from years of work and neglect. Nails stained black with grime, calloused knuckles and swollen joints. He felt immense sadness for the woman. But what could he do for her? Nothing. Joe knew that. He knew Mary was doomed and nothing he could do would stop it from happening.

"I'm sorry, Mary. I really am. I'm sorry what happened to Liz, Catherine and the others. But we need to find Druitt and his wife; they may have some answers for me. And you need to help us."

CHAPTER THIRTEEN
BEDLAM

Within its new vessel the creature waited snugly. A snippet of information here and there would help its pawns along a little. It could wait a little longer. It waited for the moment when it would reveal itself to the players in the Game. A game that it would win, a game in which freedom was the prize. And very soon it would suck that prize from their minds...

Joe led Mary, Eddows, and Flo out of Dorset Street and onto the main road. The sight was like a bright jumble of images thrown together on a canvas by a drunken artist.

During the day, Dorset Street and the surrounding area seemed much more alive than at night. Sellers and traders hawked their wares from wooden crates and boxes; small children, some wouldn't have been long out of nappies, played in the gutters with glass marbles, dodging the horses and carts that rumbled down the filthy street.

Men lounged around corners smoking and drinking. For the first time since they had arrived, Joe heard the sound of laughter and happiness despite the grime and decay of the place around them.

At least that thing doesn't come out during the day, he thought to himself. He then had the satisfaction of watching Eddows step into a fresh steaming pile of horse poo and the appalled look on the boy's face was priceless.

Once they had reached the Commercial Road, Joe allowed Mary to take the lead. She seemed to have pulled herself together and led them quickly out of the East End and into the great heart of the city itself.

Joe, Flo, and Eddows marvelled at the teeming city that surrounded them and without the trappings of the 21st century, the historic buildings seemed grander and more impressive somehow. There seemed to be less of the pollution that grimed the walls and stones on some of the buildings they recognised from the present day. In fact, Joe was quite pleased that he recognised so many of the buildings that still remained in his time, although so many of them had become hidden by the modern world, hidden by brash neon signs and bright lights. They crossed the River Thames to get to Southwark, looking down on the bustle of the river with the jetties crammed with boats. Joe couldn't believe that people could make a living fishing in the filthy water and the smell coming from the effluent was appalling.

Arriving in Southwark, Mary directed them towards a large building in the vicinity of St George's Fields. The teens stared up at the immense and imposing building in front of them. It seemed all windows and red brick. As solid as the prison it would, in time, come to represent, and seemingly twice as large, it dominated the skyline, leaving trailing shadows on the floor.

"How do we get in?" breathed Flo, staring up at the vast bulk of the asylum that lay before her. "We can't just waltz up to the door and ask for a chat with the poor woman."

"We don't need to," smiled Eddows smugly and he pointed upwards. "Look at the windows. Notice anything?"

Both Flo and Joe squinted up at the windows far above them, shielding their eyes from the bright sun.

"They've no bloody glass!" Joe squeaked. "Jeez, must be brass monkeys in the winter."

Eddows smiled condescendingly at Joe. "Probably is. The bricks are ridged, so we should be able to climb the wall and get in through the window. Mary, you need to distract the guard on the door and give us time. Just… just don't get yourself arrested."

Mary gave a small grin and nodded briefly. "Good luck," she whispered, giving Joe's arm a gentle squeeze as she slipped towards the main arch. She seemed almost carefree as she skipped in and out of the shadows towards the gatehouse.

"Stupid, just stupid, her acting like that." Joe murmured to himself. "Mad, that's what she is. She'd fit right at home in here."

Flo watched her go and then turned to Joe. "We mustn't, whatever she's done, be too hard on her," she said. "She wasn't to know all this would happen. Besides, whatever happens, she will die. And at least she's trying to make amends. Even if she has gone a strange way about it."

"I know," Joe muttered grimly as he turned his attention towards the wall. "But what can we do? We can't change the past, so we can't stop that thing. Pointless, that's what all this is. Pointless."

Flo and Joe were glad that they'd done 'bouldering' at school as they found the climb relatively easy going. Eddows, on the other hand, wished that he hadn't forged the note to get him out of PE. His head hurt and he was feeling a little sick, but he put it down to an irrational fear of heights. Joe and Flo encouraged him onwards and upwards until they reached one of the empty windows about halfway up the side of the huge building.

Clambering through, they found themselves in a long featureless corridor. Joe looked back through the window to see the form of Mary Kelly being turned away and escorted by the guards at the door to the gate. She looked up and Joe saw her face framed by the afternoon light of the sun like that of an angel. At that moment, the boy wondered if he would ever see her alive again.

***

"This is like one massive public bog." Joe led the other two down another corridor keeping low to the wall. There was no one around but the sounds of loud screams, shouts and groans told them that Bedlam was very much alive beneath them. The two boys were ahead of Flo, about halfway down the passage, when she suddenly grabbed them both by the collar.

"Stop! This is all very well and good, but what are we looking for? We don't even know this Druitt's wife's name or if she's still here. And what she flaming looks like. Whose mad idea was this anyway?"

"Mad? We're in the nut house!" Joe tried hard to suppress a giggle but failed, which set Eddows off too. Flo couldn't keep it in either: Seeing the other two rolling around the floor in hysterics, she also gave in to the hysteria, which had been bubbling around in all of them.

"Oh, that's priceless! Three nutters in the asylum!" Flo wept as the three lent against the corridor wall, spent and aching from the laughter. "What do we do now, if we can't find her?"

"They must have a records library of who's in here," Eddows, serious again, suggested. "The Bethlem Sanatorium, to give it its proper name, is an old institution, so I imagine its records will be pretty thorough. But, but how to get in there without looking suspicious? Jeans are a little suspect, don't you think? And as for that 'belt' masquerading as a flannel you're wearing, Flo, that will never do."

Joe looked hard at Eddows. He knew he was clever, but all this information was just a little too much. A nasty feeling began to gnaw at the back of his mind but he pushed it to one side to concentrate on the job at hand. Eddows was right. They'd look more than a little suspect in t-shirts, jeans and in Flo's case, goth clothing and makeup.

"I think I know just how to do it," Flo smiled cheekily and pointed to a door marked Assistant Warders.

Wearing the coats of Bedlam's orderlies that they had found in the unlocked store cupboard, Joe, Flo and Eddows sauntered down the halls of the most famous lunatic asylum in the world. It was a feeling that wasn't lost on Joe. *This is nuts*, the boy thought to himself. *Here I am, a boy from the 21st century walking around the nut house in the 19th century. It's barking, just barking.* Corridors smelling strongly of carbolic soap supressing, but not entirely eradicating the smell of urine, stretched endlessly ahead of him.

He really wished he could see Mr. Lusk's face when he confronted him about his essay on Victorian London. He couldn't help smiling to himself. For once he'd be historically accurate. Well, he would if he and the others got out of this alive.

After what seemed like an age, Eddows motioned the little group to stop. They peered through a glass pane set into a door and saw a large room filled with narrow wooden shelves full of what looked like patient files all neatly set out in order.

"Bingo!" smirked Eddows. "This, my friends, is it!"

Without a pause, Eddows swept open the door. The smell of dust and age rose up to meet them as they sneaked into the room. Joe looked in wonder at row upon row of stacked files. As he hated reading, so many books were beginning to make him feel sick, and anyway from the look of some of them, they hadn't been read or looked at in quite some time. He watched as Eddows marched directly towards one of the shelves and picked up a file.

"Got it! Lucy Druitt." Eddows brought the file over to the others and opened it up on one of the desks in the room and leafed quickly through it. With a little cry of triumph, Eddows banged it shut and smirked again.

Joe's nasty feeling resurfaced again and tiny warning bells were beginning to jingle in his head. This was all too quick, too perfect. How the hell did Eddows know where to look for all this information? It was like he had a sixth sense or something.

Before he could give voice to his misgivings, Eddows had propelled Flo towards the door. Flo turned back and motioned for Joe to follow them. With a lurching, sick feeling in the pit of his stomach, he followed.

Eddows led them with surprising speed down the gleaming corridors until they arrived at a wide iron door with a grill set into it. Large metal bolts secured the door, giving it a feeling of power and bulk. Eddows pulled open the resisting grill and they peered inside.

The smell hit them first as they peered into the gloomy room. The walls padded and thick, the floor, hard, unforgiving concrete. There was a long, narrow bunk that they supposed was a bed, and a metal pot underneath that must have been the toilet, from which, Joe supposed, the smell was coming from. Other than these solitary items, the room was unfurnished.

A woman was sat on the floor in the middle of the room. She wore a strait jacket that pinned her arms around her, but her body wasn't still. It was rocking slightly from side to side like a child's toy that had been knocked off balance.

Through the gloom, Joe could make out long, matted hair and a thin, pinched face with a mouth that was wordlessly mouthing something. Joe strained to hear but the woman was silent. It was at that moment she lifted up her head and looked straight at them through the grill.

Her eyes were black and cold and seemed to bore into them. All the horror and anguish of her predicament were reflected there. It was like looking into the swirling eddies of an icy river. Without a word, Eddows pulled back the bolts and swung open the door.

Eddows and Flo slowly approached the woman, but Joe held back. He wanted to test out the suspicion that was now deeply rooted in his mind. He reached out his hands for the metal bolts on the door...

Flo and Eddows crouched quietly down at the feet of the rocking woman. Flo looked into the woman's eyes. There was nothing there but swirling darkness; a swirling, endless darkness that seemed to go on and on into the depths of her very soul. Flo shuddered and felt her body go cold. She wondered why she was here. They would get nothing from this woman. Mrs Druitt was no longer there. Her mind was gone, lost in the endless night that was consuming her.

Flo looked again and saw to her astonishment that tears were running down Mrs Druitt's face and the rocking was increasing. Flo tried to calm the woman, but she was now rocking so fiercely that nothing could stop her.

"Mrs Druitt?" Flo asked. "Mrs Druitt, can you hear me?"

"She can't answer you. She's not there any longer." Eddows' voice cut through the silence. His voice sounded hard and calm and far away. "She's retreated into the very recesses of her mind to try and find some comfort. Some safety. But she'll find none."

Joe heard him too and moved his fingers so that they were around the bolts on the door. He tried to move them, but he couldn't budge them more than a few inches. They were stiff and hard. There was no way that Eddows could have opened the door so easily. He wasn't exactly the athletic type. Then there was the folder of information. He'd have never found it if he hadn't had some kind of prior knowledge, some given understanding of what to look for.

"Flo! Move! Move over here!" Joe's voice was hoarse and choking. Flo turned and looked at the boy and saw that his face had gone white and he was staring beyond Mrs Druitt to Eddows who was stood in the shadows on the far side of the room. She spun round to see Eddows levitate towards the ceiling and hang there like a dirty great spider. Mrs Druitt made a sound deep in her throat that became a high-pitched whimper and she tried to bury herself into the floor.

"Well done."

Eddows' voice was like a knife being scraped across metal. Flo saw the tell-tale vapour emerge from his mouth and twist in the air like black snakes. The temperature in the room dropped and the pressure increased. She felt that she couldn't move.

111

"Well done, Joseph Druitt. Who's a *clever* little boy then? Who guessed my little plan? Who would have guessed a simpleton like you would have worked out my nice little secret? Not as stupid as you look, are you?" The words hissed and steamed around the room, penetrating Joe and Flo's skulls like red-hot pins.

As Flo looked on, the shadows behind Eddows seemed to change shape. Tendrils of darkness formed the shape of a tall hat and a winged collar, a shape that would forever be linked to the stain on East London that was Dorset Street and the area it represented.

"Ripper! I thought something was wrong when Eddows went straight to the right file for Mrs Druitt and then when he managed to open that door. He'd have never managed it so easily unless he had some special help."

Joe was doing his best to keep his voice level, but Flo noticed that it was higher than usual and there was a slight shake in it as he continued.

"Why'd you bring us here?"

"So you could see. See what I can do." The voice coming from Eddows sounded proud.

"Look at that wreck of a woman there, this part of your pathetic family tree." An arm shot out from Eddows at an unnatural angle to point limply at Mrs Druitt.

"I did that. I made that. I took something that was full of life and hope and I emptied it. There's nothing there now. Just a husk of so-called humanity. Or so I thought."

Eddows floated down from the ceiling on writhing shadows and seemed to glide towards the stricken, sobbing Mrs Druitt who cowered away like a frightened animal, trying to burrow into the wall.

"Don't touch her!" Flo screamed finding her voice at last.

"You don't understand yet!" Eddows' head snapped round 180 degrees at her at an unnatural speed. So fast Joe thought the head would fall off.

"You cannot change what has already happened. You know that... *I* know that. Even I would think twice before interfering with the past. Now, the present and future is another matter. More correctly, *your* present and your future."

The creature that was Eddows smiled almost fondly at Mrs Druitt's shaking form. The smile, though, was like ice. The head swung round like a snake to face Joe.

"That is why I need you, Joseph Druitt."

Joe began to suddenly laugh. Flo looked in horror at Joe. What was wrong with him? Had it all become too much and had he finally cracked? A cry of what seemed like rage came from the Eddows creature and Flo saw a look of what seemed like anguish cross its features. Whatever Joe was finding funny had angered the thing inside Eddows and it wasn't happy.

"Brilliant!" Joe held on weakly to the doorframe. "That's just brilliant. You bring us here and show us your 'power,' but the truth is, the truth is, you are just as much trapped as we are here. Even more so."

"What, what do you mean, Joe?" Flo croaked at the boy.

"It's shown us what *has* and *is* happening in the past but, and here's the best bit, it can't change the past because if it does, it won't know what damage it could do to itself in the future. All this misery and fear, all of it true and God knows it's terrible and

113

all, but that's just it. It is all past. It can't be changed." Joe paused and smiled at Flo. A weak smile, but a smile nonetheless.

"And?" Flo wasn't sure that she quite understood.

"This thing...this Ripper, feeds on fear and misery. It's feeding on everything that is happening here now and it wants to try and feed on the fear and misery of our time. Except it's not strong enough to break free into it. It would have broken free by now, except Druitt must have found some way to stop it somehow and keep it within the stones and bricks that are Dorset Street. The blood from the six women was all it could kill—the Contract, if you like. It can influence the lives of others through possession and feeling but only that. It's bound here; its power is limited. It wants to be released."

"So? So, what?" Flo's patience had reached its end. "That thing can still kill us here."

Joe smiled triumphantly at the Eddows creature. "That's just it. It can't. Can you? We're not part of that Contract, that pact. We're not part of the past."

With a howl of rage, the Eddows Ripper threw Joe against the wall. The shadows deepened and became thicker round Joe's neck, like the tentacles of an octopus. They began to squeeze...

"You stupid little fool!" The voice blazed from Eddows throat like a raging fire. "You have no idea who you are dealing with... The blood contract with the women gave me limited freedom, freedom to work as I once worked during the Plague. I used Mary and the others to get you here and what do I find out when I probe your worthless little minds? That you know nothing of any worth to be able to give me my freedom! You and your useless friends!"

Joe just smiled. "For once being ignorant seems to have worked," he grunted.

"I want freedom! I want to be free!" Dismay and weariness had now crept into the voice. "So long, so long imprisoned within the past, with no form or shape. Inhabiting those with no hope, weak, useless, and now forced to inhabit the very stones that make up that cradle of filth from which you and your scum kind are born."

"What are you?" screamed Flo at the shape within Eddows. "What are you really?"

"I am many things, little one." Flo watched with mounting terror as Eddows' head turned three sixty degrees to look at her, like something out of a horror-film.

"I have always existed. Not just on your world but on many others throughout the multiverse. And I am not alone. There are others like me who seek to gain a foothold here in your reality and we have done many times in your past. And there have been those like you, foolish enough to try and stop us. Those like this wretched woman's useless husband. Weak he may have been…" Here the grating voice held almost a trace of respect. "But stupid he was not. His power as a warlock may have been poor, but never before have I been bound so well…that book held power beyond my understanding." Eddows' eyes rolled like filthy marbles in his head and his mouth foamed like a rabid dog, dripping glowing saliva and drool onto Joe's top. "What you see now is only a fraction of my power. I need… I NEED… I WANT the key to my release." The voice howled in anger and frustration; threatening to burst the boy's eardrums.

115

"You still haven't answered the lady's question," Joe mocked despite the pressure to his throat. "I'm Joe, pleased to meet you. And you are?"

"I am Dorset Street. I am Ripper. I am Abbadon."

"You're a muppet," grunted the boy. "You can't even kill me."

"You have no idea how much I ache to smash you out of existence, you filthy human scum!" the thing snarled, grinding Eddows' teeth together.

"I need to know why you are, were, so important to Mary. Witch or no witch, she knows something about you, which is why you were allowed to be brought here."

"Shut up. You sound like something out of *Star Wars*, or something."

"DON'T MOCK ME!" Eddows' voice rose to a shriek and his grip around Joe's neck tightened.

"Go on," choked Joe, "Do it... do it and we'll see what happens."

The Eddows Ripper's eyes burnt icy blue, horns began curling from the side of Eddows' head and more glowing foam fell dripping from its mouth and began bubbling on the floor. The thing wearing Eddows' shape, began to drag Joe with its tentacled shadows around the cell, slamming him into corners and onto the ceiling and floor.

Suddenly, Flo found that she could move. *The Eddows Ripper must be using all its power on Joe*, she thought, *and it's forgotten all about me*. She ran forward to help but found her hand grabbed by Mrs Druitt. She turned and looked at the woman's frightened face. The woman still said nothing but held her other hand at her stomach. She rubbed it once and then put her finger to her lips to indicate silence.

Flo's eyes widened and then she understood. She understood what the Ripper wanted. The key to its release was Joe.

CHAPTER FOURTEEN
LET IT OUT

"Stop!"

Flo's voice burst from her throat louder than she had expected. "Stop! You can't hurt us here and you know it. So stop all this pretence of even trying to kill us now and let Eddows go."

The Eddows Ripper released its grip on Joe's throat and turned and glided towards Flo. Tendrils of shadow wafted around her, caressing her with darkness. The sickly green, blue glow intensified around Eddows' face and the shadow of the Ripper, the top hat and high winged collar, loomed large on the wall behind.

"Release me…" The voice wheedled around in her head. "Release me from the stones that bind me here. Then we shall have peace. Then we shall be free."

Black eyes bored into Flo's as the girl stepped forward, as if hypnotised, towards the possessed boy.

Joe looked up from rubbing his neck. He was stiff and sore but that was all. His whole body ached from the savage assault by the thing, but he was still alive. He looked at the Eddows Ripper hanging above the floor like a monstrous bat, its shadows surrounding Flo and wondered what it was doing. It wasn't hurting her like it had him, it must…

"No!" screamed Joe as the sickly blue light from Eddows' mouth began to flow towards Flo. The girl tried to turn her head, but the shadowy tentacles gripped her neck and arms like a vice. Joe realised that the creature was now planning to inhabit Flo and Eddows. If that happened, whatever the creature wanted, he would use the pair as hostages. If it couldn't kill them maybe it could torture them for all eternity…

Joe had only ever been good at sport at school, so he did what came naturally. He rugby tackled the possessed Eddows from behind. The creature had been so busy concentrating on Flo that it had let its guard down and the body of the boy went over like a sack of potatoes.

A bloodcurdling scream came from the centre of the shadows that flew hazily around the room like smoke from a fire. The centre of it blazed its sickly blue colour and the whole lot shot upwards until it hung, like some filthy miasma, in the corner of the cell.

Joe looked at Eddows. The boy was white as paper and his breathing was ragged, but his eyes were back to their normal colour, and a faint smile of triumph was on his lips.

"Free," the boy whispered. "I'm completely free this time. It's gone."

Flo ran over to join the boys, dragging Mrs Druitt with them. The four of them faced the writhing shadow; one still cowered, the other three were defiant.

"What have you done?" The voice of the Ripper shrieked at them all inside their heads.

"You think you can stop me from my release? You have achieved nothing here. The same as I, *you* cannot change anything here! I thought if I possessed your minds, I could find the key that will free me from this torment, rip the information from your minds…but there is nothing! You are nothing!" The shadows seemed to expand filling the cell.

"Ah, get over yourself," Joe had had enough. "You've had it! Mary will…" The words were out of his mouth before he could stop himself.

"Mary! Ah, yes! The Contract that binds her to me… Her life is mine! She sold herself out to me! I shall take her and extract every last scrap of information I can from her. I shall be free!" The voice rose to a triumphant scream inside their heads.

Flo, Eddows and Joe watched as the opposite corner of the cell began to shimmer and appear to blow inwards. It looked like an dirty oily stain spreading across water, growing larger and more solid as it did so. It was then Eddows realised what it was.

"It's a portal!" he screamed above the babbling voices and the roaring sound that was coming from the oily stain. "The Ripper is going to portal jump and kill Mary now! We've got to stop it!" He ran forward to block the portal as the shadows swarmed eel-like towards it.

"No! Edward!"

Eddows' head jerked round. Joe never used his proper name. "You can't stop it from killing Mary. If you do then the whole of history from this, that point on will change! Don't you see? Come on, you love Doctor Who! No interfering in history. That's why it couldn't kill us! Even this thing, however powerful, can't change time in case it destroys any chance of it ever becoming free. It needs us to get to the present, to our time, where the future hasn't yet been written."

"But we must find out where it's going now, or we won't be able to stop it back in our time!" shouted Flo over the raging storm. "We have to pass through the portal with it."

"Look out!" roared Joe as the Ripper shadow bore down on Eddows and the portal. For the second time in minutes, Eddows found himself rugby tackled to the floor and felt the ice-cold sweep of the Ripper as it passed over his head and into the portal.

"After it!" screamed Flo "We can't lose it now!"

"What about her?" shouted Joe looking at the prone figure of Mrs Druitt. "We can't just leave her here. Not after what's just happened."

Flo looked at the figure of the troubled woman, hair flying wildly in the eye of the portal wind. As she looked, Mrs Druitt stood up straight, her hand still on her stomach. But there was something different now on her face.

A strange, sad smile that held resignation but also, what was it? Hope? Lucy Druitt nodded at Flo who turned and gripped Joe's outstretched hand. The boy held out his other hand for Eddows who came and gripped it firmly. Then, as one, the three jumped into the churning portal.

***

The threesome turned away from the dirty window that looked into what had been Mary Kelly's home. The portal had led them through to the location the teens had come to know as the only safe place for them in this miserable age. Eddows stood grim faced with Flo while Joe was sick against the wall. Although the body of the dead woman had been taken away, the police had not yet bothered to clean the blood from the walls of the dwelling. The creature had done its terrible work well.

Joe felt terrible. He couldn't understand how anybody, or anything could kill in such a horrific way. He held his aching head against the cold, wet window and let out a racking sob. Once he started, he found that he couldn't stop. Wave after wave of grief and anguish leaked out of him and he began to beat his fists uselessly on the rotting wood and brickwork until he felt his own blood mingling with the dirt. He hadn't known Mary well and still didn't fully understand why she had brought him here, but he understood all too well the poverty and misery that had been her life. And yet she still had hope that there would be something better—and now she was dead.

Eddows and Flo watched pale faced, as Joe tore at the rotting stones and wood. They didn't stop him. If Joe could go and tear down the entire street in his rage and grief, then so much the better: if he could destroy the very stones that imprisoned the Ripper and end forever its legacy of horror and misery, then let him do it. It was only when Flo saw the blood coming from Joe's hands that she gently pulled him away and held him tight.

Noticing Joe's mood, Eddows slumped down by the door and held his head in his hands. He was thinking, thinking hard. The whole thing was a mess. What was more he felt guilty about letting the creature take him over. But then he probably couldn't have stopped it, he reasoned. He had to move on and try and redeem himself by solving the riddle. It was like a giant puzzle that was made up of so many parts it couldn't all be put together as they all seemed to be holding different pieces. The only thing that was clear was that, whatever the Ripper really was, it must be stopped.

Flo let go of Joe as she felt his sobs become less. Joe let out a long breath and looked up at her with a dirty tear stained face. "We've got to stop this thing, whatever it is and send it back to hell."

"That's it!" Eddows looked at them both. "We need to send it back. To hell or wherever it comes from. We need to find the last missing piece from this jigsaw. We know that Jack the Ripper doesn't kill again, so maybe now will be the time that we can stop this thing."

His fingers clenched making fists as he remembered the icy fingers of the Ripper manipulating his brain, making him do terrible things. "However, I'm sick of not knowing the whole picture and I think Druitt knows. We've got to find him. He let this thing out and was able to bind it—so he can send it back."

Joe's face fell. "That's all very well, Eddows, but where the hell are we gonna find him? London is a big place and we ain't got no sat nav."

"I know." Flo's voice made the boys turn. "I've been there before. It's the place where Eddows got possessed."

CHAPTER FIFTEEN
ABBADON

Joe gripped the handle of the window fastening and pulled hard. With a protesting groan, it began to turn in his hand, bits of rust and grime falling onto the splintered wooden sill. With a final wrench and a muttered swear word from Joe, the window opened and the three peered into the gloomy interior.

It had taken a long time to find the place where Flo had first met the Ripper creature. She wasn't sure she would've been able to, but through careful probing from both boys, they had located the grim terraced house, on the corner of a typical East End street.

"Ladies first," smirked Eddows and held out his arm for Flo to take. "As everything seems to be happening to either me or Joe, it's about time something happened to you."

"Pig." Flo smiled cheerfully and, taking the proffered arm, jumped down into the room and took a good look about her.

The place was cluttered and jumbled. Dust and cobwebs hung over the place as if it hadn't been cleaned in a long time. There were easy chairs covered in deep red throws that had seen better days and a rickety table with some cheap tin plates and cups. On one of the plates there was the remains of a slowly decaying meal, half a loaf of mouldy bread and some rotting fruit swarming with flies. Chipped wooden floorboards were covered with old rugs that were threadbare. A large bookcase stuffed and crammed with old books, scrolls and rather horribly, a human skull, dominated one of the walls. A stargazing chart hung next to it, curling at the edges. In front of it was a long bench laden with glass bottles and phials holding strangely coloured liquids and powders. *Druitt was obviously into magic and alchemy big time*, thought Flo to herself, and then jumped as a rat ran over her foot and into the frayed base of the easy chair.

"What's wrong?" Eddows' voice, full of concern, came down to her from the window. "You all right?"

"Fine." hissed back Flo. "Come on down and take a look." She heard two thumps as the boys landed on the wooden floor behind her. "Look at this lot. And avoid the rat."

"Whoa!" gasped Joe as he looked over the range of equipment on the bench. "It looks like old Druitt was well into his hocus-pocus. Looks like he was really into all this stuff." He picked up a phial of greenish liquid and shook it gently, then choked as a pungent smell wafted forth.

"Which means," said Eddows, who had already begun to poke around the bookshelf, "We might just find something to explain this mess to us and then we can work out what to do."

It was sometime later that Joe threw the chair across the room and watched with grim satisfaction, as it had broken apart in a splintering crash. He always felt better smashing something.

They had found nothing and despite some new and interesting smells that came from the large glass jars and phials that he had tried mixing together, there was nothing of any interest. What made it worse for Joe was that he couldn't read any of the stuff in the books that was interesting the other two.

"Found anything yet?" he asked moodily.

"Not yet," replied Eddows calmly. He knew how Joe must feel but decided that it would be better not to dwell on it and just carry on. "Lots of stuff about Jewish demons, time corridors, moon phase conjunctions and magic, but nothing that would help us. Looking at these books though, it does appear that he really believed in all this mumbo jumbo."

Joe's mouth hung loosely open. He had no idea what Eddows was talking about.

He turned away knowing he'd get nothing from Flo who was curled up on one of the dusty chairs, deep in concentration over a book that was almost as large as her. Joe wandered over to the stargazing chart that hung down over the wall and tried to feign some interest in it. On it the constellations swirled and eddied like stones dropped in a lake. Planets and stars hung in orbit around many suns that made no sense. It was beautifully drawn, but it didn't mean anything. It was just a pretty pattern. One that drew you into it…much like one of those magic eye pictures he was so rubbish at. *Maybe if I look hard enough*, thought Joe, *I'd find that flaming dolphin.*

It was at that moment that he felt sick again. Sick much like he had felt in the car park that had once been Dorset Street, sick like he had felt at the site of the murders. He felt dizzy and leaned forward to support himself on the wall and felt himself falling forward, ripping the chart off the wall as he pitched into a doorway hidden right behind it.

Joe felt his friends' arms pick him up off the floor and heard Flo gasp out loud. He tried to focus, and images began to swim into view before his eyes. A deep hollow room filled his vision. It was like a deep pit. The floor was littered with the bones of both humans and animals, all in various states of decay. It was horrific.

It was the room of Flo's nightmare.

They edged further into the room, taking care not to tread on the bones that crunched like dry leaves under their feet. Flo noticed the archway she had crouched behind before and motioned the other two to follow her through. The room widened into an arching chamber.

This one was different. It looked like something out of a film set designed by a maniac. Unlike the novice books and rudiments of alchemy they had seen in the Druitt's living room, this was a full-blown shrine. Great heavy tomes bound in leather were lined up on stone shelves across the wall; strange astrological charts and weird symbols hung from the ceiling. Lanterns made from animal skulls lit the horrid scene with an odd green light. What made it worse was the ugly looking altar at one end of the shrine.

A low stone altar covered in bizarre signs and symbols, writhing tentacles, fish and odd-looking creatures that did not exist anywhere on earth sat in the centre of the room. On the altar was a large red book, surmounted with a golden star, covered in runes and archaic symbols that seemed to draw the attention of the threesome to it. It seemed strange and not of this world.

That must be the book that Mary was talking about, Joe thought to himself. The book that had been given to her by that green-eyed man, whoever he might be. *It wasn't Mary who brought me here. It was the green-eyed man.*

Set around the floor, as if cutting the altar off from the rest of the room, was a pentagram drawn in a dark brownish paint.

"Blood." Eddows voice echoed hollowly around the chamber as he knelt down by the pentagram. "Mary and her coven's seal with the Ripper. Fat lot of good it did them."

A small desk was at one side of the room and on it lay a small battered diary open on its last entry. Flo picked it up and began to thumb through it. Most of it was dull boring stuff she couldn't be bothered to read, so she flicked through it towards the end. She gave a small cry that startled the boys as they inspected the shrine.

"I had found the last piece of the puzzle…" Flo started to read.

"Get her!" interrupted Eddows.

Flo slapped his arm hard. "Not me, you muppet. Druitt. This must be his diary." She continued to read, slowly at first and then faster with ever mounting excitement and horror.

"I had found the last piece to the puzzle. The door between two worlds. Some women came to see me today. They had discovered some old writings linked to Jewish scholars during the time of the Great Plague and wanted to know more. They were somewhat uneducated, so I agreed to translate the writings for them. It was more than I could have hoped for. They had found not only the writings they spoke of but also a book of what seemed like ancient Kabbalistic magic. I agreed to perform a spell for them as a sign of my gratitude. It appears they had formed a sort of primitive coven. Who am I to refuse them?"

Flo stopped reading and eyed the two boys. "Only a man could be so stupid to muck around with something he doesn't understand to impress a bunch of girls."

"Get on with it." Joe wanted to know more and not being able to read it himself, needed the girl to do it for him.

"My wife begged me not to continue, but I was insistent. I hoped that all my research into alchemy would culminate here, leading me into being able to transmute lead into gold. They arrived around an hour before midnight.

"After a cursory reading of the text it became clear that a covenant between us all and the spirit world would be needed. I had thought that this part at least, was mumbo jumbo; if only I had listened to Lucy!"

"I had found this sanctum behind the wall to my home where I would perform the ceremony. I found it by accident when I was doing some work erecting my bookshelves. The mortar holding the stones behind the shelves was rotten, and when I pushed through the room behind was revealed. What it was doing there I do not know. I assume it is the remains of some older, more primitive structure."

Eddows and Joe stared at the shrine. It had felt otherworldly before, but now it positively radiated with an ancient primal evil that seeped from its very centre. An evil that had existed since the dawn of time. The air around them seemed full of whispers. Whispers of the dead, and those who had taken part in the rituals around the shrine, that was steeped in the blood of ages past.

Flo read on. "We began the ceremony by mixing our blood on some of the stones of the building, to keep whatever appeared bound to this world. I used my own to anchor the ritual to the book. That part, it appears, has at least worked. I then called on the spirit, Abbadon, to come forth to our reality and show itself. And it did, with all the powers of hell.

"It spoke through my wife, using her as a vessel to communicate with us. It told us it had walked our earth before us and would do so again. Never again would it be bound in stone. It did not realise that the blood of a few would do so; when it found itself held again, it vowed revenge."

The three looked at each other. Their feeling of terror grew and gnawed inside them like the rats that scurried and burrowed around the room. When they had thought of Jack the Ripper, they had always thought of him as a man, a truly terrible one, but a man of flesh and blood all the same. Now what they were dealing with was something different: something impossible to comprehend in the 21st century with its e-mail, i-Pods, and MSN. They were dealing with an embodiment of pure evil. A demon. A demon from another dimension.

"So… what is this Abbadon?" asked Eddows. "This demon Druitt's conjured up, there must be some information about it. Anything in that diary?"

Flo skimmed the text, mouthing as she read and finally, she let out a cry of triumph. "Here it is! Abbadon: the old Jewish word for Place of Destruction. Given form as that of the Destroying Angel of the Pit… oh great! Now we're dealing with a major demon. Not just a mini one but a bloody great big one!"

Eddows looked thoughtful. He didn't believe in demons, at least not the Biblical sense, and the appearance of the "holes" in space kept coming back to him, intriguing the budding scientist within him.

"To me, this Abbadon is some creature from another place, another dimension. A world that must be very different to our own. Our ancestors had no understanding of space and time like we have and called it a demon. You know, like thinking there was a god hammering away inside a volcano."

Throwing a loose stone at the shrine and finding satisfaction when it met with a resounding crack, Joe grunted moodily. "Give a name to something they don't understand, eh? A UFD. Unidentified Flying Demon."

"Exactly. Who's to say these creatures haven't been trying to gain a foothold on our reality throughout time. Look at our mythology. Sea creatures, gods, monsters. All of it seems silly to our world but take a sideways look and it all makes perfect sense."

Eddows rubbed the side of his nose and looked at the other two who were just staring at him. "Well, makes sense to me anyway. Is there anything else in that book of yours, Flo?"

Flo looked with renewed interest at Eddows. He was so clever and so handsome; those eyes and those cheekbones... She felt herself blush slightly and read on.

"Well, Doctor, it seems that Druitt was able to imprison Abbadon within the stones of Dorset Street using the power the book possessed and using his family name. He chose this street, as it was a place of extreme poverty and misery, likened to hell already. He didn't realise that all the suffering and vice that went on here would eventually give it energy, power and form..."

"Which is why and how they got the Ripper!" shouted Joe finally linking the puzzle pieces together. "And because the girls had sealed their Contract with it with blood, they were the Ripper's chosen victims! Oh, it all makes sense now!"

Suddenly the triumphant look went out of his eyes and he slumped forward onto the altar. "But that still doesn't explain why we were brought here and how we can stop it, does it?"

"I think I know why. Druitt was, is, the Ripper's physical body in that things' hunt for his Contracts. He used Druitt to murder the girls as the Ripper."

Joe and Eddows turned and looked at Flo. Her face had gone pale and her hands were shaking as she held the diary in her hands.

"The last entry from Druitt." She began to read, her voice trembling as she did so.

"I go to face this thing that has used me for its work. Used me as an instrument of death and made me kill those women against my will. I will banish this fiend back to the hole from which it crawled or die in the attempt. No longer will I serve evil. After all I have Lucy to think about and a child on the way."

"Lucy Druitt was pregnant when we saw her in Bedlam, wasn't she?" breathed Eddows. "Druitt must have found some way to shield her blood as another Contract of the Ripper. If it had killed her, a descendant of your family now…"

"Then in the future I wouldn't exist. It wouldn't risk killing me because it wouldn't know what damage it could do to itself in the future if I wasn't around. Am I right?" Joe shuddered at the thought.

"Sounds vaguely plausible to me. As Mary and the other girls had no children, their family lines stopped. This has been planned all along for decades, even down to you being here. As for by whom, I have no idea."

I do, thought Joe, *and he has green eyes*.

"All we have to do is to find and help Druitt and get him to send us back leaving the past as it was, erm, is. Simple!" Eddows was saying as he shoved his hands into his pockets and started towards the door of the shrine.

Flo called him back.

"No! Eddows, Joe! You don't get it! The only way out for Druitt to be free of Abaddon is to die

CHAPTER SIXTEEN
THE BRIDGE BETWEEN WORLDS

The threesome stood outside Druitt's burning house looking up at the tongues of flame that licked and curled around the dark beams. Already shouts and cries came from the other houses nearby as people ran to and fro with buckets of water trying to put out the blaze. Nobody took any notice of the teenagers who stood with upturned faces watching the inferno.

With a roar of flame and splintering of blackened wood, the roof of the dwelling, which had held such evil and seen such misery and horror, fell in, sending a shower of sparks, like glowing stars into the cold night sky.

It was Joe who had made the decision to destroy all the wicked things Druitt had collected. He had felt fire would at least cleanse part of London from the stain of the Ripper and there had been some comfort in watching the stuff burn. But they were now confused and very frightened. They knew they were dealing with not just a human killer but a demon, or whatever it was, from another time and place, and from its display of power, a very strong, determined one. A demon that wanted to be free.

"We've got to find Druitt." Flo tried to focus them all on the task ahead of them. "He must be somewhere nearby. We don't have an all-purpose underground yet. He can't have got far."

"Well, actually the Central Line was completed four years ago," started Eddows, before Flo kicked him hard in the shins for trying to be clever.

"It never runs to time anyway," quipped Joe. "Besides, it's all pointless as we don't know what Druitt looks like properly, do we? Only a few glimpses of him being sick at each murder. There were no photos of him in the house either or any drawings, not that we could go back and look."

Another shower of sparks followed by a plume of thick black smoke came from the burning house.

"We don't need to," Eddows murmured. "He's already a wanted man. Look!"

The other two followed his gaze and their eyes fell on a badly drawn poster, clumsily pasted to a wall. It was tattered and dog-eared but still readable. Flo went closer and touched the rough surface. It came away in her hand.

"Montague John Druitt. Wanted in possible connection to the murder of Mary Kelly and several others in the Whitechapel area…"

Flo sagged against the wall and clenched her fists. Eddows turned away in disgust with the thought of how Druitt must be feeling, being used as a puppet against his will, by a heartless monster.

Joe began to feel hot tears welling up in the corners of his eyes and an immense hatred for the thing that had possessed Druitt. He hadn't known Mary well or long, but she had treated him with kindness in the hostile and cruel world in which he had found himself. It wasn't fair! He could picture her smile in his head, her laugh, he could almost hear her voice…

"Joe! Oh, for gawd's sake, Joe, I'm over 'ere!"

He could hear her voice. Joe turned his head and squinted down a dingy narrow alley adjacent to the main street. It was almost dark now and the night was closing in like a blanket, but at the end of the alley, he saw her.

Mary Kelly. She was shadowy, indistinct. Her hair and clothes were moving as if blown by an invisible wind; a green-blue light glowed around her. He motioned to the other two and they approached the shade.

"Mary? Is that you?" Joe felt stupid for asking the question but so many strange things had happened that he wasn't sure of anything anymore.

"Yes, Joe. It's me, took yer bloody time answering. Don't be sad. You knew before all this happened that I was going to die. Don't come as a surprise. It ain't so bad 'ere with me and the girls. All together again."

Behind Mary, indistinct and shadowy, like reflections in glass, Joe and the others could see the forms of five other women. They seemed to wave at them, as if through smoke.

"How… why are you here?" Eddows cut in. "You've shown us the Ripper and what it really is. Now what do you want? We want to go home." He ended huffily.

"You need to find Druitt, don't yah?"

"Yes," admitted Eddows. "But what I don't understand is, why we had to come and see all this death…this murder. Couldn't we have just been told about it by you in our own time if you can travel from place to place?"

"And deny you the real 'arsh truth of it all? You 'ad to find out what the Ripper really is. I couldn't tell you as it might 'ave changed things before they 'ad happened. What you know now, it will 'elp you defeat Ripper in the present before it destroys it and yer future...opening the doorway for others of its kind."

Mary looked sadly at the trio. The ghostly form of her and her friends had become even more shadowy and thin. They were now little more than stains in the air.

"Joe," she said gently, "It'll be down to you..."

Joe looked with horror at Mary as her shape dissolved on the wind into dust.

"Please, not me! What can I do? I can't even read!"

"Seek out Druitt at the bridge before midnight... the greatest bridge of all London... before midnight."

Mary's voice was lost on the wind and her form faded from view, somewhere a clock struck the hour and the darkness was complete.

Flo rubbed her dry lips and leaned against the rough wall. "London Bridge. Got to be. That's where Druitt is. But why the bridge?"

"Don't you remember what you said back at Druitt's house?" Eddows asked. "You said that the only way out for Druitt was to die. And what is London Bridge famous for?"

"Traffic jams?" offered Joe, puzzled. He became even more puzzled when Eddows smacked him on the back with a groan.

"No! You meatloaf! Suicide! Druitt's going to kill himself!"

***

The trio ran hard through the dark and foggy streets of Victorian London following the tall spire of Big Ben and the glow coming up off the river. On and on they ran, up steep slime-encrusted steps and the darkened alleys that hid the shame of the great city from the eyes of the world.

Soon they had left the squalor of the East End behind them and they found themselves pounding down the last mile towards the great bridge that spanned one of the most famous waterways in the world. Yet at this time of its life, the dark smudge that was the Thames was polluted beyond endurance and nothing much lived in its foul, stagnant, and cold waters. A fitting place for an encounter with a demon.

With lungs fit to burst, they paused at the entrance to the massive stone structure that towered above them in the ice-cold air. London Bridge soared away into the darkness dizzying them as they craned their necks for any trace of the elusive Druitt.

Joe glanced at the elegant structures of Big Ben and St Paul's Cathedral, which were so familiar to him, and tried to make out the time. It had taken them precious minutes to reach the bridge. He even found himself wishing for London transport. It was five minutes to midnight.

As the boy stared at the clock, faint flakes of snow began to fall, gently at first and then with increasing intensity, spinning through the chilly air like tiny, crystallised diamonds.

"There he is!" shouted Flo and pointed at the faint form of a man sat on one of the buttress-like sides of the great bridge.

They ran down the length of the bridge as the snow fell harder and harder and became a raging blizzard, whiting out the rest of London.

Druitt's small, black form was like a dark beacon in the dazzling white and as they got closer, he turned his lank-haired head to look at them. No sound penetrated the whiteout and Flo felt herself as if in a tunnel.

"Stay away!" His voice was surprisingly strong in what appeared so small a form. "Don't come any closer. Don't…"

"It's all right, Druitt. We know who you are." Flo's voice sounded high and cold in the swirling snow. "We know who you are and what's happening to you. We…we can help you." She realised how pathetic she sounded but she had to try.

"You know nothing about me!" Druitt looked directly at them and the three of them gasped in horror. Druitt's features were pale and distorted like a melted wax candle. His face was white as the snow that was falling. His mouth was a black gash in the sugar white skin and hung open at an ugly angle. The eyes were red rimmed and sunk deep into his face. The pupils were black like a bottomless pit and all trace of the whites around them had gone.

"Look at me!" Druitt screamed at the three and threw back his hair to reveal the beginnings of horns that were curling from his skin, black and leathery. The shadowy form of the Ripper superimposed itself over Druitt.

"Now tell me what you know!"

The voice changed again and again as the words repeated themselves, first in the human voice of Druitt and then again and again in the rasping, cruel voice of the otherworld, of the so-called demon, Abbadon.

"Abbadon! That's what we know about you and what you are—Ripper."

The ugly features seemed to soften slightly and the eyes regained something like humanity.

"Then let me do this. Help me…" Druitt held out his arms to Flo who stepped forward. "Help me!" The voice changed again, soft and gentle. Persuasive even: persuasive and evil.

"No!" Eddows grabbed Flo's shoulder and held her back. "That's what it wants. I wonder just how much of Druitt is left in there. It won't be any part that is sane."

"Help me," Druitt held out his arms. They moved jerkily, like a muddled robot. "Give me freedom. Give me my freedom!"

Joe noticed the fingernails on Druitt's hands were becoming like talons, curved and cruel, getting longer, even as he watched.

"Help who? Druitt or Abbadon? Which are you really?" Eddows snapped at the form in front of him, remembering how he had felt possessed by the monster. "What's left of Druitt? Have you consumed him completely or is he still in there somewhere? Well?"

The thing that wore Druitt's shape chuckled throatily and looked again at Flo.

"Come inside and find out," it slobbered, still staring at the girl with hard, black eyes like obsidian.

Flo flinched as a cruel and cunning smile now began to play on Druitt's lips and the voice that spoke, although coming from the man's mouth, didn't fit with the movement of the lips.

"Well done, boy." The voice sounded like nails scraped across a blackboard. "Druitt is in here with me, just not able to respond. Chained like he chained me. Soon I will have suppressed him completely and he will be mine. His soul consumed forever. His shell, a husk for me to control while his soul is forever bound to the pit for all eternity. I think that the cosmetic changes to his form are already favourable."

A curling talon reached up and gently patted the curling horns that were sprouting from Druitt's head. A shudder of revulsion ran through Flo and she felt for Joe's hand.

"Then why are you here, if you control Druitt so completely?" asked Eddows.

"A mere oversight on my part, nothing more. I had other, erm, business to attend to which left Druitt able to make a small break for freedom." The Druitt creature looked sharply at Joe and there was almost respect in the voice when it spoke, "The woman was brave. She put up quite a struggle. She died well."

Eddows placed a restraining hand on Joe's shoulder.

"But over Druitt, I now have complete control. He will not die. At least not his physical form. I will continue to use him, not only here, now, but in your time too. I will be able to preserve his body until I can take possession of something more... suitable. And now, we can all travel through to the present, *my* present together." The creature let out a low chuckle and looked back along the bridge into the swirling darkness.

"What do you mean?" Eddows said curiously.

"The portal to your time will only open once on this particular night, but it needs your simple friend's aura to open, things from the time it will lock onto, a meeting of past and present so to speak."

Eddows remembered what Mary had said about using an item from her time, her violets, to allow her to appear in the present.

"The boy was born in this area, unlike you two who come from further down the river. So, I allowed you to find me to ensure that the portal will open in what will be the area of Dorset Street in the present."

The Druitt Abbadon demon smiled, the features unnatural, like the sweaty makeup on a clown beginning to run. "And once I am through, I need no contract to kill, to rule in your time. The

140

hatred, fear and despair built up in this city over the millennia will be a contract enough. And soon, when I am finished with London, I will consume your world."

The snow began to billow harder now, thick like feathers, forcing the teenagers to shield their eyes from the storm.

"Do you know what day and time it is here? New Year's Eve! The end of the old and the beginning of the new! An apt portent, don't you think?" The demon creature roared in triumph as the sky around the bridge began to flicker and distort like a melting mirror. A sound like a million grinding gears heralded the arrival of the time vortex.

The shape-wearing demon pointed a talon at Joe and smiled.

"It comes! The portal comes! Do you hear? You were a key, boy, nothing more! But now that it is here and the present and past are joined as one, I no longer need you alive! Any of you! There will be no damage to the timeline!"

With startling speed, the Druitt creature charged at the three bringing them crashing to floor. Eddows felt his head crack hard onto the stone buttress behind him, making him feel dizzy and sick. He shook his head and saw Flo trying to drag Druitt's arms away from Joe's throat. With one clawed hand, Druitt threw her to one side and continued to squeeze, even as behind them the snow began whirling into a corridor that glowed and pulsed with light.

The Druitt demon took one triumphant look behind him and increased his hold around Joe's throat. The corridor became more solid, real and the wind increased, screaming with an unearthly fury that threatened to pull down the bridge on which they fought. Eddows knew that they only had one chance.

"Druitt!" he screamed above the melee, "If you're still in there, do what you set out here to do! Finish this here and now and send this creature back to whatever hell it comes from!"

Eddows saw the Druitt creature briefly relax its hold on Joe's neck and the boy managed to struggle free. Druitt began shaking from side to side, clutching his head in his hands, pulling pathetically at the horns on the side of its misshapen head.

"If not for us, then do it for Lucy!" bellowed Eddows.

"Yes! I must do it! For my wife! I'm not a monster! I'm not!" Druitt's own voice resonated from the wracked, tortured body. The screaming man tottered over to the edge of the bridge and looked down, poised to throw himself into the unforgiving depths. Suddenly the body unnaturally back flipped away, and the face had changed to that of Abbadon. The eyes became jet black once more and stared with hatred at the three teens, face the colour of a gutted fish, more inhuman than ever.

With a casual wave of an arm, the demon sent all three flying into the stonework of the bridge and held them there, squirming like eels, with invisible restraints.

"You little fools!" the voice full of hissing snakes bored into their brains once more.

"Do you really think you can stop me? This is my time! My freedom!" With another wave of its arm it began to throw them around like rag dolls against the walls of the bridge.

"Druitt! What about your freedom! You deserve better than this! Better than being some vessel for this…this thing!" Eddows' voice rose above the storm and Joe could see a momentary glimmer in the dead eyes and the form of Abbadon over Druitt clutched at its shadowy head.

142

"Free! I… will…be…free!" Druitt's own voice rang clearly over the driving snow and wind.

He began to clamber painfully up and over the side of the bridge. Joe, Flo and Eddows watched as the horrid scene played out before their eyes as the shadow of Abbadon clawed at Druitt furiously trying to increase its hold over the man. But for once, in the last moments of his lost life and soul, Druitt the man prevailed over the demon. With a last desperate effort, he pulled himself upright and looked down at the swirling water that whirled and eddied below him in the dark.

Raising his head, Druitt took in the scene; the raging time corridor and billowing snow, beyond the shape of the great city of London and the three battered and bruised teenagers. Tears formed in his eyes and ran in torrents down his ravaged cheeks. The voice that came from his torn mouth was, at long last, his own.

"I never meant for all this mess. I couldn't stop it once it was released. I can't stop it now. But…" he turned and looked at Joe. "You can, boy. You'll know what I mean when the time comes, and the streets become dark and rise again. Do it for me, for the women I've killed and for the wife I've lost. Do it!"

With a cry that rang high into the night, Druitt dropped like a stone into the freezing waters of the Thames. Joe, Eddows and Flo watched as the waters closed over his head and he was seen no more.

The teens had barely let out their breath when the waters exploded upwards showering them with dirty, freezing icy droplets as the black spirit of Abbadon, the Jewish Demon of the Pit and the Ripper of Old London Town, came shrieking from the water.

"You stupid mortals! You cannot stop me!" The screaming voice tore through their ears and into their brains. "I cannot be stopped by you destroying that puny vessel. I shall use the very stones that imprisoned me to crush you and your miserable world!"

With a roar of rage, the spirit flew like an arrow into the heart of the time vortex and was gone. Momentarily stunned, the trio watched it go. Joe shook his head. Something in him still didn't believe what was happening.

"Come on, we've got to stop it! Let's get after it!"

Galvanised into action the three ran and jumped into the heart of the storm, hot on the heels of the Ripper.

***

The darkness was complete, and Joe wondered if he was dead. Maybe the time corridor hadn't worked, and he was dead. Then he realised that maybe it would be a good idea if he opened his eyes. He slowly forced them open and the world swam back into focus. It was a strange world that he was looking at. Grey and hard… like concrete.

It was concrete. His face was nose to tarmac with the ground. Joe blinked again and felt a weight on his back. A weight that groaned and wriggled: a weight that sounded very much like Eddows.

"Get off me, you great lump!"

Joe heaved the prone boy off his back and immediately felt lighter as Eddows crashed off him and onto the floor. "Trust you to find somewhere soft to land."

Joe slowly sat up rubbing his sore and battered body and flexed his arms and legs. He then looked around him. Eddows rolled over and lay on his back and grinned at Joe.

"We're home. I never thought I'd miss concrete so much."

"You didn't land on concrete."

"No. I landed on something soft and flabby that absorbed the impact of the landing. You landed on the concrete. It's still good to see it though."

Joe couldn't help smiling back at Eddows. Even after all that had happened, it felt good to be home. He looked around at the by now familiar car park. The dirty electric lights, the zigzag lines and the yellow spacings on the concrete floor. All so safe, all so normal. And yet... and yet something was missing. Joe couldn't quite put his finger on it.

"Flo!" shouted Eddows, sitting bolt upright. "Where is Flo? She came back through the time corridor with us, so where is she?"

Joe felt the blood drain from his face and a sickly dry feeling enter his mouth. A slight scuffling sound made both boys turn and look at a familiar, dark shadow that squirmed with unnatural life underneath the car park doorway.

And in the doorway was Flo. She was struggling against the seething black mass that threatened to engulf her. Flo managed to pull the darkness away from her mouth long enough to shout a warning at the two boys before writhing tentacles of shadow shot out from the mass and slammed into them, knocking the breath from their bodies. When both boys opened their eyes again both Flo and the shape had gone.

CHAPTER SEVENTEEN
HOME

"Great, just bloody great," moaned Joe as he and Eddows jogged quickly down the main street towards Joe's flat. "Now what do we do? That thing's got Flo and we haven't any idea how to deal with it. I blame you."

"Thanks," Eddows gasped sardonically as they turned into the Joe's street, narrowly avoiding the car that nearly went into the side of them; at least they hadn't had to worry about traffic in Victorian London, other than the odd horse and piles of poo.

"Thanks a bunch! After all we've been through and you're still moaning."

The boys climbed the stairs of the tower block two at a time until they reached Joe's flat. They had no idea what they were going to do but at least they would be safe. Joe opened the door, kicking the built-up newspapers and take away leaflets out of the way, and calling out to his mum and nan at the same time.

"Mum! Nan! You there? It's me, Joe. I'm back! Sorry I haven't been in touch lately! It's been a bit manic. Mum? Nan?"

Silence.

The hairs on the back of the lads' neck began to rise as a hissing, giggling chuckle issued forth from the living room.

Joe kicked opened the door and froze. Eddows bundled into him and both boys stared at the scene in front of them. The whole room was a mass of moving, writhing shadows that reached

146

upwards draining the very light from the room. Joe's mum, nan and Flo were held tightly by coils of pure shadow.

"Welcome home, Joseph Druitt."

Abbadon's voice rasped from the heart of the shadows. "It's so good to be back and meet some old faces. I've just got reacquainted with your nan here. Although I have to say, the conversation has been mostly one way. She doesn't tend to say very much, does she?"

Joe felt his hands ball into fists. He didn't mind this thing attacking him but his family! And especially his nan! What could a harmless old woman mean to it? And then it hit him. All the pieces of the puzzle fell into place; Dorset Street, Mary Kelly, Druitt... all slotted into place.

"Nan," he whispered. "You're Druitt's daughter, aren't you? You've been hiding that secret all these years. And now it's out."

"It's all in the family," muttered Eddows. "That creature has no interest in me or Flo. It's you it wants; you and your family."

"Oh, you're wrong, boy," chuckled the demon darkly. "Revenge for my imprisonment does not interest me now I am free. All of you belong to me. Now. All of you and your filthy kind are descendants of those who would imprison me. And now I will consume this world and take control and the streets of darkness will live again!"

"You need a vessel to do that!" Joe shouted at the crawling shadow. "What I don't get is why you haven't taken one of us here already."

"Why should I limit myself to a prison of flesh? Druitt was weak, flawed. Human," hissed the demon from the centre of the shadowy web. "I shall take a new form. One that is much more

147

fitting for a destroying angel of the pit! And it shall be the last thing you see before you die!"

Instantly the room became completely dark and the demon was gone. The lights in the room flickered and came to life. Flo slumped to the ground rubbing her raw wrists and moving her jaw around. Eddows ran to her and sat cradling her. Despite the makeup he was taking a shine to the girl.

Joe's mum was leading his nan over to her chair and Joe realised now just how old she really was. As he looked at the tiny, frail woman, he noticed a determined spark come into Nan's eyes: a spark that he had seen before in Druitt's wife just before they had left her. He wondered...

"Nan?" he asked quietly. "Nan? Can you help us stop it?"

"No, Joe!"

Joe turned and saw his mum looking with anger at him and felt himself flinch. He'd never seen his mum look at him like that before.

"It can't be stopped. If it could, don't you think we wouldn't have kept it a secret from you all these years? We knew what the Ripper really was. I knew you'd been seen at the Ten Bells Pub. I bet you wondered why they all looked so scared when they saw you, eh? They all know about Joseph Druitt. All passed down from mother to daughter over the generations. Why'd you think you don't have a dad, eh?

"The Ripper can only possess a male form. You were a mistake! Can you imagine the danger to us all if you had been taken over by that thing? So, we kept you from it all. It was the only thing to do."

Joe stood opened mouthed looking at his mother. He felt hurt and crushed. He was a mistake! An accident, he was something that wasn't supposed to happen—that was how his own mother felt about him. He felt Flo's light touch on his shoulder and Eddows' arm leading him towards the door when a light dry voice stopped him.

"No, Joe. You are no mistake. You were meant to happen."

All three teens turned and looked at Joe's Nan. However frail she might be, the old lady stood unbowed from the recent events. She shook off Joe's mum's restraining arm and settled herself down in her chair. To Joe it was the most serene he had ever seen the woman.

"Your mum doesn't mean it, lad. She's just frightened and well she might be, but listen to me now, you are no mistake."

Joe's mum's mouth opened and shut like a fish out of water and she slumped into the nearest armchair. She began to rub her arms nervously up and down as if she was cold.

"You are a special boy, Joe," went on the old woman.

"The Ripper, Abbadon can't possess you as you are the Chosen One."

Joe thought back to all his encounters with the thing that called itself the Ripper. Every time it had tried to frighten him, upset him and scare him away, it had never once tried to take him over. It was almost as if it were scared of him and what he meant.

"She's right," muttered Eddows. "It only possessed me and tried to possess Flo."

"You alone can defeat this monster. Your mother was too scared and frightened to admit you could do it. But you can, and you must!"

Nan held her chin up defiantly at him. "You will." For a second Nan reminded Eddows of Churchill.

149

Joe felt his head about to explode and he fell with a thump, heavily onto the sofa and held his head in his hands and shook himself hard. He didn't get it and he wanted out. He heard Flo talking softly to Nan.

"Why, Nan, is Joe so special? What has he got that can defeat this thing?"

"Ever wondered why you can't read?" the old woman's voice bored into his brain. "Ever wondered why, whatever you tried to read, it all came out garbled? It's because you can read a hidden language that only you can see and understand. It would be no good me or your mum trying to help, even if we wanted to, as the gift you have could only be passed on through a male link from Druitt himself. As to why you are so special, I don't know."

"That's just it!" exploded the boy leaping up out of the chair and making the others in the room start with surprise. "I don't know who I am! No one ever told me! You never did! No one ever helped me once! Never explained why I couldn't! Never told me that I wasn't a loser! Never once told me that I was clever or special! You never even spoke until now!"

Nan shook her head gently and smiled sadly at the angry boy in front of her then held out her arms to him. Joe fell sobbing into the old lady's embrace and held her tight. Joe's mum, unable to bear it any longer, went over and hugged them both. As the tears subsided, Nan carried on.

"I couldn't talk until today. Not proper anyway. My mother, as you must know, was sent to Bedlam. She was never released and died there. I was taken away at a young age and given up to the parish that housed me with a family. They told me when I was older about my mother and what had become of her. One day, when I was about the age you are now, I was visited by a man who said that he was from the parish council and had found some of my father's things and that he was returning them to me."

"Who was he?" Eddows asked.

"Don't rightly know. Just remember very green eyes,"

Joe gulped but said nothing. Green eyes…They had enough to deal with at the moment.

Nan continued, "One of the things, amidst a load of junk was a book. From that moment on, I couldn't speak, it was as if some magic had been released that silenced me and kept me apart from the world. I was made to marry; I had children and expected to die. But no… I went on. I watched my family grow old and go to the grave around me while I went on."

"Then that makes you…" Joe tried to do the maths and then gave up. "Well over a hundred years old! You ain't my nan, you're my great-great nan!"

Nan gave a tired smile and nodded.

"Big family secret! Took some convincing the NHS on the family's part that I'd died and been buried abroad or at least chucked over the side of the boat! My granddaughter had your mother here. I wondered why I carried on. I knew it had something to do with that damn book, but I never had the nerve to let anyone look at it. Not even your mother here. Felt there was too much in it that could do us harm. Couldn't read it anyway."

"Where is it?" Joe asked. He felt desperate to see it but didn't know why.

"We'll get to that in a minute. It was only when you were born, all those years later, the first male descendent of Druitt, that I was visited by Mary Kelly."

"Just like we were," whispered Flo. "She told you then?"

"About the Ripper. About Abbadon. About everything. Yes, she did. She also told me about Joe and his gift."

She held up Joe's face to her own with gnarled hands that smelt of lavender. "And now, Joe, you must use that gift you've been given and send that bloody creature back to where it belongs!"

"I see where he gets his language from," Eddows mouthed to Flo gently and then to her surprise took her hand.

CHAPTER EIGHTEEN
STREETS OF DARKNESS

Nan motioned them all to follow her to her bedroom, a riot of orange and yellow swirls that hadn't been repainted since 1975. Joe helped the old lady into her room where she fumbled about under her bed and brought out an old book. Eddows glanced at Flo. They both recognised the book at once; they had seen it in Druitt's shrine. It was blood red with a golden star. It was the spell book.

"This book, Lord knows where it came from, was used by your great, great and I imagine a few more greats, grandfather to summon the demon, creating a contract with it. The book must be powerful, as it's kept me silent and prolonged my life, for what it's been worth; what can work for evil can also work for good," explained Nan to Joe and the others.

"And now you, as the only direct male link to Druitt, must use this book to send it back!"

"Nan, I can't read," Joe said as Nan without a word, pushed the book at him. He went to hand it back, but the old girl was insistent.

With a sigh, Joe reached over and opened the book.

Flo and Eddows craned their necks to try and read it over his shoulders, but they couldn't make out the strange symbols or writing. Weird pictures of creatures and people littered the pages. It meant nothing to them and they both shrugged their shoulders.

Then, to their surprise, Joe started to laugh and laugh. He was laughing so much he had to hand the book to Eddows for fear of dropping it.

"I can read it!" coughed the boy, wiping his eyes and clutching his sides. "Oh, that's priceless! I can read it and you lot can't!" He flumped down on the side of Nan's bed and dabbed his eyes with a particularly vivid piece of eiderdown with the pattern of a peacock on it. "Sorry," he gasped to Nan as he saw her looking a little disapprovingly at the soggy peacock.

"All right, clever clogs, give it a rest." huffed Eddows, ever so slightly peeved. "What does it say? How do we stop Abbadon?"

Joe took the book back from his friend and read the words set down so many thousands of years ago by who knew what inhuman hand. He ran his fingers down the pages flicking and turning them over with the novel sensation that he could read them and everyone else could not. He finally found what he had been looking for. "At its source; only can the demon there be bound and defeated and sent back to the dark pit from which it came." He snapped the book shut with a bang and a little cloud of dust. "Well, we all know where this demon's source is, don't we? Dorset Street."

They all suddenly started as a noise came from outside. A scream rent the air, followed by another and another. Something big was going on.

"Out!" cried Joe jumping up from the peacock eiderdown and running to the doorway, "Stay here!" he shouted to his nan and mother as he, still clutching the book, ran from the room followed by Eddows and Flo.

The three stared at the incredible and bizarre scene that was unfolding outside the flats and houses of the East End. Amidst the running, screaming crowds of people, crashed cars and buses, one thing transfixed the view of the trio.

In the place of the car park that marked the resting place of Dorset Street buried so many feet below, trapped in the slime and the mud of the past, a transposed image of the same street hung above it. But this was not the still image that Joe had seen before. This one was stretching, growing, changing shape, becoming alive as it did so. Joe watched as the street pulsated with a black light and, at its centre, the same sickly blue-green glow that he had seen so many times before.

Tendrils of writhing, filthy darkness twisted through the air, steaming and pulsating with damp, death and decay. Everything the tendrils touched became dark, stained with evil and corruption. As the tentacles curled round the few trees and bushes of the East End, they shrivelled and died.

Dorset Street lived once again.

The tendrils flowed on, destroying all that they touched, like the disease and contagion the street had once represented.

It's like the end of the world, thought Eddows to himself, as the present began to be consumed by the past.

As he watched, more tendrils reached out touching the fleeing people. As they were caressed by the darkness, their eyes became blank and staring and blue glowing mucus fell from their limp mouths.

Zombie apocalypse, the boy thought.

Joe noticed people he knew transformed into blank-eyed living dead. Busybody Mrs Patel, who by the look of her shopping bag had just bought more wool for knitting those hideous scarves he always got given for Christmas, Debs the kind lady from the Council, the irritating identical Sanderson twins, old Mr Smith, and even his arthritic dog, Amber. More and more were touched by the darkness. Miss Thompson, recently arrived from Greece, dropped the kebab she was holding, while Mr Miller from upstairs ripped off his velvet smoking jacket and joined the blank-eyed throng, spewing black shadows as he did so.

A foul, dank smell filled the air mixed with another more sulphurous one that rankled the back of Joe and the others' throats, making them cough and retch. Like the stain of the past before it, the tendrils of Abbadon didn't care who they touched. Young, old, male and female fell to the darkness. They turned on those not yet caught by the stain, turning them into more of their number.

Evil, mocking laughter came from all sides at once.

"It's corrupting them all! It's taking them all over!" screamed Flo, coughing above the smell of the acrid gas that streamed and floated towards them, threatening to overwhelm them with its stench.

"Then it's time it stopped!" roared Joe and before the others could stop him he charged into the heart of Dorset Street, knocking the flailing zombie hordes aside, noting the balls of yarn and wool that fell from Mrs Patel's shopping bag and thinking he'd have to pick it up later, and into the very form of Abbadon. Flo and Eddows made to follow him but found their way blocked by a dead-eyed Mr Lusk who spat blue bile at their feet.

"And he tells us off for spitting! Talk about hypocrisy!" Flo quipped as they looked at the advancing form of their history teacher.

"No time for a lesson now," muttered Eddows. "Much as the thought of physical activity fills me with horror, let's try a little rugby!"

With a cry, that he wished didn't sound so much like a baby having its nappy changed, the boy charged shoulder first at his possessed teacher followed by Flo.

***

Inside the street all was still and silent. Joe looked around and let out a low whistle. It was like stepping onto a film set. The silence was deafening. Joe made his way down the silent street. Suddenly the ground lurched underfoot, throwing the boy to the ground. Mocking, evil laughter filled his head.

"Welcome to hell!" scratched the voice in his mind.

Like a living horror film, the decaying brickwork and buildings took on the living embodiment of all the souls of those it had consumed over the many years of its terrible existence. Broken faces that were full of pain, misery and sin, screamed out from the crumbling tenements and flats. Grey, spindly arms formed out of the brickwork and reached out to him, imploring him to save them from damnation. Joe stumbled away from them and stopped dead in his tracks. At the far end of the street, waiting for him, was an all-too-familiar form.

A scratch of darkness stood at the far end of the street.

A long buttoned-up coat and a top hat perched on top hiding all trace of the unspeakable face underneath, ever-present black horns clearly curling underneath the brim. Its long shadow reached towards him pulling him in. Daring him to enter.

The Ripper.

"Brave, I'll give you that, boy. Brave and stupid, coming here into my domain!" The voice shrieked in his head like rusting hinges.

"You don't scare me," hissed Joe. "Hiding behind that shadow. Show me what you really are. Or are you really that ugly?"

A long, high laugh came from the form of the Ripper and it began to change before the boy's startled eyes. It grew and grew consuming the houses and walls of Dorset Street around it. The doomed souls of its lost inhabitants becoming part of the awful, growing thing that was materialising before him.

The hat and coat were ripped from the demon's head and back. Cruel claws shot out of powerful, muscular arms; a blue scaly body that glowed with an unearthly light; legs that ended in thick cloven hooves fringed with rough, coarse looking hair. A pair of huge, leathery wings unfolded from the back of the monster.

But it was the face of Abbadon that riveted Joe's attention. He had seen glimmers of it in the agonies of Druitt, but this was worse than anything he could imagine.

A grotesque parody of the human face surmounted by curling ram horns over a goat-like face. Eyes that poured out blackness like death stared down at him. A mouth full of jagged broken fangs opened in a sickly attempt at a smile and a black, forked tongue ran across the thick blue lips sending viscous blue foam raining down upon Joe.

"Now, do you see, little one? Now do you see just how helpless you are?"

Joe felt, rather than heard, the voice that bored like a laser into his brain, but he felt the claws of the creature close around him and lift him up so he was level with it's awful face.

Sulphurous steam oozed from its nostrils set in a sharp aquiline nose as Abbadon gazed at him. Joe tried not to choke and turned his head as tears welled up from the corners of his eyes. The face that he stared at was one of pure unsullied evil. A face that had existed for millions of years before humanity was even born: a face born among stars and countless planets and places unknown. It was cold, passionless, and dead and it gazed with curiosity at the boy.

Joe felt he was looking at the devil himself.

"A pity, really, if this is the best your world can manage. You were never any match for me. A fool is all you are, a stupid little fool." The demon's voice was casual, purring even, as if Joe really didn't matter at all. "Look upon me and weep, little boy. See me as I really am."

"What are you?" the boy managed to gasp through the pain and the thick steam that threatened to choke his lungs. "Where are you from?"

"I am from a universe and time beyond your imagining, child. I am older and more ancient than your primitive world. I am beyond your understanding. See…"

The blank eyes opened wide and Joe felt himself falling into their black depths.

Space and time swam before the boy's eyes and Joe saw the demon free of its earthly prison. There was something almost beautiful as Abbadon opened his bat-like wings wide and soared among the stars. *An angel of the pit*, thought Joe. That is what he was: an angel of the pit. Joe watched as the demon flew past planets, nebula and hidden universes. The boy was mesmerised. Maybe he'd been wrong about what Abbadon was. Maybe…

Joe watched as Abbadon reached a small planet. Blue, green, lush with vegetation, plants and animals: a world of plenty. The boy could see and feel the strange inhabitants of the world below looking up from prosperous cities and towns at the demon that loomed over them like a monstrous shadow. He felt their fear and their pain and screamed within his own head.

Abbadon reached out his arms. Ribbons of darkness stretched forward, writhing and twisting like the dragons Joe had loved hearing about at school when he was young, as an escape from everyday life. Except these dragons dealt with death.

They encircled the world until only darkness remained. The people and the cities turned to smoke and ashes and the world turned to dust and only space remained. Joe felt his eyes stinging and he fell backwards into the demon's eyes once more.

"That is what I am, little one!" came the voice in his head.

"I am a destroyer of worlds and consumer of souls. And I will suck this world of yours dry and leave it dead."

The voice was casual as if all of this was of no importance to the demon. No compassion, no pity. Just death. "Give in child," came the voice of the demon. "I will wipe the slate clean. Cleanse the universe, your universe, your world of all the anger, poverty and despair and leave it as nothing. Your world will burn in cleansing fire and all will know peace."

Joe felt a rib crack as Abbadon began to squeeze him harder around the waist. Images began to flash through his head. Images of his mum, nan, Eddows, Flo, Druitt and Mary… Mary… Mary. She had believed in him. And now he would end up like her, dead. Killed by this monster.

Suddenly his flailing fingers touched something stuffed into his pocket. He moved them again against the agonising pain the demon was causing to his body; it was Druitt's spell book. An image of green eyes scratched across his mind.

"Use the book!" A deep, rich voice echoed in his head above the noise of the triumphant demon. The green eyes flashed again.

With a mighty effort, Joe wriggled the book free from his pocket. The cover and pages felt reassuring in his hand. He then rubbed the little book against the giant blue hand that was crushing him. The effect was electric.

The demon screamed as if it had been burnt by fire and released its grip on Joe who fell heavily to the floor. Joe watched as the creature turned its massive horned head, looked at its burnt, blackened hand, to again look at him, and saw a fleeting flame of something different in its dead eyes: fear.

"You have the book!" Joe felt the voice like a knife in his head. "Where did you get it? It is not of this world! The book that summoned me and then bound me to the pit and place from which I came! You will not use it!"

"Ah, dry up!" Joe had heard enough. "Taste some magic!"

But before he could speak any magic words from the tome in his hands, Abbadon had raised its massive arms and sent the boy and the book flying against the nearest wall and there they stayed trapped by the demon's own powerful dark magic and tendrils of black mist. Joe could feel the pressure on his chest increase as the demon crushed the life and breath from his body. He felt an all-consuming fire in his mouth and throat…

"And now…" said the demon with a smile that could have curdled milk and shattered mirrors, "You die." The pressure on Joe's ribs increased.

A brick hit the back of the demon's head, who, momentarily stunned that anyone would have the audacity to face it, turned to stare at Flo and Eddows who stood defiantly in front of it.

"Didn't think we'd let you have all the fun, did you?" quipped Eddows lobbing another brick at the behemoth, watching it bounce off its chest and burst into fragments on the ground. "Lusk was no match for a rugby tackle committed by a genius mathematician with an eye on angle of descent and fall."

Flo couldn't help grinning at the quip and had to admit she had been quite impressed when Eddows had taken out the history teacher.

Throwing Joe casually aside, Abbadon raised his arms and chains of darkness and decay swirled above the massive horned head.

"Besides, there's no one left to talk to out there," offered Flo. "Old demon boy's taken all the talk out of them. And they don't half have bad breath!"

"And talking of demon boy—have a bigger brick!"

Eddows flung another brick that crashed off the creature's scaly hide and then dived for cover as a tentacle of darkness ploughed into the earth next to him, showering him with dirt and debris. Abbadon swung round again as another brick delivered by Flo struck a blow to its left horn. Blue shimmering blood dripped off the wound and burnt a hole as it hit the ground. Screaming with rage that anyone would dare attack it, the demon shot bolt after bolt of darkness at the pair who drew it away from Joe.

Joe shook himself to and sat up on the floor, as he watched the distracted demon being tormented by his friends. Now where was it? Joe scrabbled among the rubble and found the spell book that had been knocked from his pocket when Abbadon had thrown him.

Rubbing the grime off the cover and opening the book, Joe looked at the words on the page. He started to read through them in his head and then stopped. What if it didn't work? He heard a cry as Abbadon pinned Flo and Eddows with multiple black tendrils.

"Read it, Joe!"

Mary Kelly's voice echoed in his head and he looked up to see her shade in front of him. As he stared at her, other shades appeared next to her; the other victims of the Ripper: Martha, Annie, Polly, Catherine, Lizzie, Druitt, and his wife. They all were there willing him on. He felt tears pricking his eyes. They believed in him, these shadows from the past. As he looked, more ghosts or shades appeared, wearing clothes that stretched back further into the past. Joe could see Roman armour, Tudor outfits and what looked like a medieval knight among the ghosts.

All victims of the demon, Abbadon. All victims of an ancient evil. They were here and ready to stand with him. Joe wouldn't let them down.

He began to read it aloud, the words tumbling out of his mouth like a torrent. He had no idea what he was reading, but he kept on. The book began to glow in his hands, brighter and brighter until he could barely look or read the words, but still he kept on and on.

"Azal, demoni cataclzymal! Binderous Abbadon eterinous…" His voice grew in power with every word.

Abbadon turned and saw the boy and the glowing book and screaming with rage and frustration, released its hold on Flo and Eddows who crashed like the bricks they had been throwing to the floor. Tendrils of darkness flew towards Joe but dissolved into nothingness as they touched the light.

Joe saw something new reflected in those bottomless pits of eyes. Something that the demon itself had loved to create. Fear.

Howling now in anger, Abbadon charged at the boy and found itself flung backwards like a limp rag doll by the force of the boy's words and land with an earth-shaking crash on the ground.

"You cannot…destroy… me!" the knife-like voice screamed in Joe's head.

"You are nothing but a little worm! You are nothing to my greatness! My symphony of darkness!"

"It looks a lot lighter in here! At least 60 watts!" shouted Joe as he continued to read faster and faster and faster. The demon began to clutch and tear at its stomach as if in pain. Steam and sulphur fell from its monstrous maw and nostrils.

Shaking its horned head in agony, its black eyes glazed in fear at the insignificant boy who finished the last line of the spell and held out the open book towards the demon.

"No! Please…mercy! Show me mercy! I only wanted to be free!" screamed the demon as Joe continued his relentless advance.

"Begging for mercy?" roared Joe, "How much mercy did you show your victims before you killed them? About as much as I'm going to show you now, I reckon! Binderous, binderous eternous eternia eternous!" cried the boy at the top of his voice.

Joe then heard the voices of all the past inhabitants of Dorset Street joining in the words in unison. The sound rose above the roaring of the now cowering form of Abbadon like that of a celestial choir singing in the heavens.

"Banish-ed destructos despondos!"

A blinding burst of light shot from the book. It struck the monster full in the stomach and went straight through the other side. Impaled on the shaft of light, the demon twisted and writhed in agony as the light took hold of it and threw it, pinned like a butterfly on a board, onto the nearest wall. Eddows and Flo hobbled over to join Joe who had begun to walk towards the twisting form of Abbadon.

"It's over, Ripper!" called the boy at the monster as it tried to claw itself free of the beam of light.

"You used all the hatred and misery in Dorset Street to kill and corrupt as much as you could. But you forgot about what made up that street. No, it's not just bricks and mortar that made it what it was, what it is: it's the people! People who care, love and fight against all that you are and all that you have become! It is over, Abbadon the Ripper. Now I'm ending this!"

And with a mighty throw, as if he had known what to do all along, Joe threw the book into the very heart of the demon.

Screaming in horror, Abbadon tore at its own stomach as the book burned into it. The trio watched as the demon began to implode upon itself, the darkness and tendrils sucked inside the crumbling body. In a last-ditch attempt to hold on to this reality, Abbadon dug its huge claws into the wall and the children covered their faces from the showers of dust and stone.

Squinting through his fingers, Joe could see the face of the beast. Abbadon's features were etched with all the pain and misery that it had caused others, and, for one brief moment, Joe was sure he could see something else deep within those eyes: a fleeting glimpse of the horror of being trapped forever in its own eternal darkness. Then it was gone as the huge face began to crumble to dust and the eyes grew dead. The enormous horns fell forward as the immense form began to dissolve into nothingness.

The claws embedded in the walls of Dorset Street fell forward ripping the walls out with it. The three teenagers dived for cover as the whole wretched street began to collapse.

"Run for it!" shouted Flo, grabbing Eddows' hand and shoving Joe, forcing the other two to tear themselves away from the image of the decaying demon. A great crack began to open in the very ground as the Street of Darkness began to topple into it. Light, flame and dust began to billow forth from the abyss, as the mouldering heap of Abbadon's body and Dorset Street fell into it.

Joe took one last look over his shoulder to see the shimmering forms of the late inhabitants of Dorset Street fade into nothingness; turning back he stumbled and, as he put his hands out to stop himself hitting the ground, a tiny posy of flowers, violets, rolled into his outstretched hand: a parting gift from his Mary Kelly.

Coughing and spluttering, the threesome charged towards the safety of the main street as the great crack in the ground began to close behind them. Looking back from a safe distance, the trio saw the hole vomit forth a jet of blue and green flame that shot heavenward. Joe swore that in the flames he could see the face of the demon, writhing and twisting in agony.

166

Then the chasm smashed shut, burying forever the demon of the Ripper and the remnants of Dorset Street.

The ground vibrated and shook as the car park rebuilt itself on top of the smouldering land. Flo was reminded of playing a DVD backwards. *An odd image*, she thought, *though not as weird as what just happened.* She glanced around her at the rebuilt present day.

"Look at all the people! They're coming out of it!" she cried.

Eddows, Flo and Joe watched, as all around, people began to shake their heads as if from a dream and carry on as if nothing was wrong. Joe saw Mrs Patel tut and pick up her dropped balls of yarn and stuff them back in her bag. Amber shook herself vigorously and gave a sigh before cocking a leg and giving the nearest lamppost a yellow sheen.

"We don't need your recommendation, thank you," Eddows said with a raised eyebrow.

The three sunk to their knees and began to laugh as if they couldn't stop. Behind them the sun peered out behind the spire of Christ Church. It was over.

CHAPTER EIGHTEEN
THE END OF IT ALL

Later, the rending of the earth had been explained by the authorities as a freak earthquake and the possession of the people said to be a release of poisonous gas produced by the quake, and all returned to normal. Complete drivel, as if anyone would believe that, Eddows had said. But they had believed it and life carried on.

It was during that week that Joe discovered something strange. He was making lunch for himself and his nan when he realised that he could read. The instructions on the back of the Smash packet made sense! He could read! Excitedly, he grabbed the nearest recipe book off the shelf and checked again. It was true! He could read every damn word! He was no longer "stupid."

Running into the next room, he swung his surprised mum around by the waist and hugged his smiling nan. Joe was still getting used to the fact she could talk and that she was "well old." How long she'd last now that the book was gone was anyone's guess, but Nan didn't look like she was failing yet, and he was glad of it. Glad that he had time to talk to her, not just about the past but about the future, too. Nan had also mentioned at least thirty times that she needed a new bed cover. She'd always hated that peacock.

"I can read!" Joe cried, jumping up and down with excitement.

"I thought that might happen," said the inscrutable Nan with a wink. "I suppose you only needed to defeat Ripper, and when you did, it released the magic bound up in you. Like scales fallen from your eyes."

She took a swig from the cup of tea balanced on the arm of the chair.

Joe's mum turned to her son. Since the end of it all she had been very quiet and almost off-hand with Joe.

"Joe…" she began slowly and falteringly, "what I said about you being a mistake. I'm sorry. I was wrong. I just wanted to protect you from that thing… I…"

Joe just hugged her. "I know, Mum. You don't have to be sorry. You were just trying to keep me safe." He swung her round again and apologised as Nan's tea ended up on the carpet of the now-spotless living room. Another change since his adventure had ended, but then so much had. Mum had found herself a new and steady job and had decided that boyfriends were not worth the bother.

***

The doorbell rang, and Joe went to answer it. Flo and Eddows stood there smiling and Joe noticed with a slight smirk that they were holding hands. They had been spending a lot of time with each other since the adventure, and although Joe had featured heavily, he had a feeling that sometimes they wanted him out of the way. That suited Joe fine as he now had the time to concentrate on his reading.

Slowly and surely, Joe was enjoying books more and more. He was also using the single cookbook he'd found in the kitchen cupboard to cook meals for his mum and nan. Sometimes he had to still feign ignorance when plumes of black smoke belched forth from the oven.

Since being back at school, Joe had surprised his teachers with his commitment and new dedication to his own education. It was as if he wanted out of the situation that had cornered his family all this time. Mr Lusk had almost passed out when he had read Joe's essay on the East End, so accurate were the details enclosed within the pages.

Joe looked at his two new friends and almost felt a surge of pride that it was his adventure that had brought them together.

"We thought we'd do it now," Eddows said and Flo nodded in agreement.

"We don't want to forget them all," she added.

"Right. Let's go," affirmed Joe.

"I'll be back for tea!" he called to his mum and nan and closed the door behind him to the sound of Nan and his mum chatting away. The sound was so right and so comforting to him now. He swore the last thing he heard as the door shut was Nan talking about changing the carpet in her bedroom to something a little less orange.

From the window of the flat, Joe's mum and Nan watched them go. Just three ordinary-looking teenage children, who had defeated a demon from another dimension and, in all probability, saved the world.

"Do they have any idea what they are?" Joe's mum asked her Nan as she turned away from the window. "Have they any clue as to what they've stumbled on? What if they find out that there's more to this than they realise?"

"This would have happened sooner or later," Nan broke in, "Let's hope that they don't get discovered. There are many who would want to test those kids' powers and use them for evil."

Nan shuddered at her own words and looked down at her cup of tea. "Like the... no, no, there can't be any of them left anymore. This world is older and stranger than they can possibly imagine."

Even as they spoke, neither noticed below them the man in a black suit and blank, wax-like face stood by a sleek black car, the door embossed with a golden star, looking up at their window. Suddenly, the man stiffened, as if radio-controlled, and moved over to the darkened window in the back of the car.

The window slid silently down as the black-suited man bent his head to the opening and listened to the instructions from the shadowy occupant inside the car. A flash of green eyes came from the velvet depths and the window slid shut. The blank-faced man got into the car, started the engine and purred away from the tower block.

***

The three teens stood silently at the altar of Christ Church as Joe laid a bouquet of flowers on the rail.

They all had a lot to thank Mary and the other people of Dorset Street for, and they felt that this was the best way of doing it. Giving back to Mary and her friends the dignity they didn't have in life.

"Do you really think it's all over?" asked Flo. "The time corridor, could it happen again? It was created by Mary and her friends to reach us, so who's to say it won't?"

171

"She's right," Eddows agreed. "The time portals could always surface again. They aren't under the control of Mary, Druitt, Abbadon or anyone. They are tuned into our auras, or rather yours, Joe! Remember what was said, about other worlds and places. I almost hope they do!"

Joe kneed Eddows in the leg.

"I mean it," the boy said seriously. "There could be other corridors and vortexes that could open anywhere. And who knows what could come through?"

The three then looked around, half expecting to be carried away, Wizard of Oz-like, by a storm at that very moment, but nothing happened. Joe smiled a broad smile. "Well, Eddows, if it does, I have you and Flo to rely on, don't I? As long as we all stick together. Although some of us are stuck a little closer…"

He winced as Eddows thumped him playfully in the shoulder and wheeled him around. Flo began to laugh, and it wasn't long before the others joined her. "We could be like the Famous Five!" she giggled.

"Five? There are only us three. I know I ain't the sharpest tool in the box, but even I can count that far!" Joe grinned at her. "But I like the idea. Chips anyone?" and the others nodded their heads in agreement.

As one, arms linked, they left the church and a stillness and peace came upon the silence. As the doors shut behind them the bouquet of flowers began to stir as if brushed by an unseen wind. Petals began to fall, gently at first, and then they floated in mid-air before being tugged in a pattern round and around as if within a whirlpool…

HISTORY

Towards the end of the 19th century, London was at the centre of the Great British Empire that covered half the globe in the name of Queen Victoria. The London where Joe and the others find themselves in *Streets of Darkness* was one of intense contrasts. The rich people of the city cared little for those who were poor, destitute, or homeless. Only a few influential people, such as Doctor Banardo, who looked after homeless boys on the streets, cared what was happening to those less fortunate than themselves.

The East End of London was one of the poorest districts in the Capital. Once the home of prosperous 16th century Dutch Huguenot silk weavers, the area fell into disuse when new trade routes opened the city up to cheaper materials and products from around the world.

The weavers' proud houses were left to decay and rot, taken over by unscrupulous landlords, who crowded people and families into filthy rooms with no toilets or running water. Rats and lice were prevalent and diseases that have all but been wiped out today, such as cholera and tuberculosis, were common. People worked many unpleasant jobs, especially around the dock area of Poplar.

The East End became a haven for Jewish immigrants who were escaping persecution and hatred in Europe. They settled in areas such as Whitechapel, Limehouse and Spitalfields using some of the buildings as their places of worship, called synagogues. One of these, Sandy Row Synagogue near Old Spitalfields Market, is still standing having been opened in 1766. The other inhabitants of the East End were mistrustful of the new arrivals and legends and myths grew up around the Jewish community, such as the story of the Golem, a mythical clay monster who would come to life when magic words were uttered and of the stranger and more obscure aspect of Judaism.

However, the East End also became a safe place for criminals and thieves who hid themselves in the maze-like warrens of the streets. Certain areas became known as "Rookeries" for the criminal underworld and became so bad that even the police would not venture there for fear of being attacked.

It was in 1888 that the area gained an even more dangerous reputation: that of the murder of five women at the hands of an unknown killer who was quickly termed by the newspapers at the time as Jack the Ripper. The murders shocked even the hardened people of the East End, so shocking and violent were the killings.

The first murder was of Mary Ann Nichols in Durward Street, just outside where Whitechapel station is now. Four more brutal murders followed, ending with Mary Jane Kelly in Dorset Street. The street itself, as noted in the story, is now a car park, which has gained the reputation of being one of the worst car parks in London!

The residents of Whitechapel were terrified that they would be next in line to be murdered by the Ripper and rumour and gossip around the identity of the killer were rife. Some said that he was a mad Jew as many of the murders carried examples of Jewish ritual and there existed a great deal of anti-Semitism against Jews in the area at that time. Another theory is that the

Ripper was a member of group called the Freemasons who committed the murders. Others suspects included Sir William Gull, physician to Queen Victoria to keep quiet the unsavoury exploits of some members of the Royal Family, and even the strange son of Edward VII, Prince Albert Victor of Clarence.

Another suspect was Montague John Druitt, a schoolteacher, whose body was found floating in the River Thames on the 31st December 1888.

After the death of Mary Kelly, the murders stopped. Jack the Ripper was never caught, and the murders became stuff of legend. The image of a black-suited, cloaked killer with top hat, bag and knife disappearing into the smog of Victorian London was the one portrayed in many film and TV programmes.

As a result of the murders, public sympathy made the government look again at the conditions of the poor in East London and more police and better lighting were introduced to the area. As the 19th century came to an end, many of the houses, tenement buildings and squares, including Dorset Street, were demolished to try and make life better for the inhabitants of the East End.

Although many of the original areas of Victorian Whitechapel have been demolished, swept away by the modern world, one can imagine, when alone on the streets of the East End of London, the voices of those who once lived there, now long dead, buried and gone, whispering and calling out of the stones, like the very victims of Jack the Ripper and his ilk, of what was termed, "The Worst Street in London," the "Streets of Darkness."